Gambling
ON THE BODYGUARD

A WHAT HAPPENS IN VEGAS STORY

SARAH BALLANCE

Entangled Publishing, LLC
2614 South Timberline Road
Suite 109
Fort Collins, CO 80525
Visit our website at www.entangledpublishing.com.

Lovestruck is an imprint of Entangled Publishing, LLC.

Edited by Tracy Montoya
Cover design by Heather Howland
Cover art from Deposit Photos

Manufactured in the United States of America

First Edition September 2015

For my husband, Ryan, who refuses to step foot on a plane for any reason. Except Vegas.

Chapter One

Ellie Montgomery's entire life had just disappeared down the toilet. Literally.

A once-in-a-lifetime event. Exclusive access. *Gone.*

She'd traveled hundreds of miles to meet Willie Focker, the hottest man to ever grace the cover of a book. It had been lust at first sight, right there in the romance section of Barnes & Noble. She'd religiously collected books featuring him on the cover but never dreamed that filling out the little card between the pages would result in her winning a ticket to meet the man in all his glorious flesh at the eighteenth annual Romance Novel Convention. Taking a few days off work and flying alone to Vegas was probably the craziest thing she'd ever done, but if she was going to do something crazy, Vegas was the place to do it, and Willie Focker the reason.

At least he *had* been.

She stared at her dripping wet hand. Had she really

stuck it *in the toilet*? Fortunately the bowl appeared pristine, but that didn't relieve the urge—scratch that, the *need*—to take a bath in sanitizer. When the ticket first landed in the water, she'd required a good second to process what was in the bowl, at which point she made a frantic grab for the paper only to have it disappear, courtesy of the auto-flush. Long after the invitation to meet the man of her dreams was lost to the sewers, she stared into the bowl, praying the darn thing would show some mercy and regurgitate the envelope, but luck did not prevail. She contemplated going in after it, the urge tempered only by the fact that she'd be in no shape to meet anyone if she drowned in toilet water.

"Un. Freaking. Believable."

With a sigh, she threw her too-small-to-hold-a-damn-thing bag over her shoulder and cursed it for not having a pocket that fit the gold embossed invitation, then for good measure she cursed the invitation for being too big for her bag yet inexplicably not too big for the hole at the bottom of the toilet. Torn between denial and utter devastation, she eased from the stall, casting a final desperate look into the bowl before the door swung shut after her.

It freaking figured. The odds of her landing one of ten tickets to what was promised to be an intimate affair were off the charts, statistically lingering somewhere between winning one of those cars at the penny slots and getting struck by lightning while spelunking in Carlsbad. That the sewer would claim her chance was just her luck.

She'd been inside the Masquerade Hotel and Casino for all of an hour, and she'd already lost her heart and soul to Sin City.

One of ten tickets.

She straightened.

Intimate affair.

There had to be a record of invited guests. Surely all she had to do was show up and give her name, and she'd be in. Buoyed by that one last shred of hope, she scrubbed her hands, then straightened her dress and her spine and headed for the venue. A concierge named Perry with a Trump-quality comb-over and a store-bought smile directed her toward the conference room that promised Willie Focker.

Outside the door, a dozen or so women jostled one another, yelling the cover model's name. A dozen voices insisted they were on the list. A dozen excuses flew to the return of a dozen nopes.

Each and every one was told it didn't matter.

No ticket, no entry.

Ellie held back. Sure, she had a ticket, but she wouldn't be saying anything the rest of them weren't. If a list existed, short of her being an A-lister or a runway model, she'd be hard pressed to get anyone to consult it. She appeared to be at another dead end, but desperation squandered defeat. Security clearly had their collective hands full, so all she had to do was find the back entrance to the room. So what if she didn't have a criminal bone in her body? The real crime would be to miss this chance to meet Willie. Rumor had it he would pose for mock covers with the attendees, which meant he'd probably be shirtless. And she'd be in his arms. It would be the closest she'd come to a relationship in ages.

Besides, she *was* on the list.

She eased around the corner from the melee and searched Google for the hotel floor plan. The conference room in question, together with its neighbor, could be converted from two single rooms into a spacious double room, and the door to the second half was off an out-of-sight corridor. She wasn't sure how the two rooms connected—probably one of those accordion walls that would be impossible to sneak through—but she'd bridge that gap when she got there.

She scoped out the hall and compared it to the diagram on her phone. Only one corner stood between her and international perfection.

"Just. Act. Casual." *And breathe.* Minor detail, but a deal breaker if she lost sight of that particular goal and passed out on the floor. But *calm* was a joke. She was just as worked up over the idea of standing face-to-face with Focker as she was by the loss of the ticket. Her emotions ran in circles, no idea which direction to take, so it was no surprise her attempt to be discreet failed. Nothing made a person conspicuous like trying not to be, but she made to the second entrance without being tackled. Brief second thoughts assaulted. She had no idea what would be on the other side of the door, but worst case, she'd play utterly confused and end up escorted to the corridor where she started. If she could just tell her story, they'd all have a good laugh and she'd be in. Willie Focker would pose for that cover with her, she'd leave with photographic proof, and it would keep her warm at night.

With her pathetic wreck of a love life, it would have to.

The short back corridor was well lit, but the inset door was thrown into deep shadow. At least if she failed miserably and video evidence made the rounds on YouTube, she could pull the *Not Me* card. But the risk was worth taking.

Here goes nothing.

She eased open the door, expecting all hell to break

loose. But other than the muffled noise from the adjacent conference room, silence reigned. *Well, okay then.* She turned to shut the door, then back around and…hit a wall.

A wall made of man. One who smelled like soap and was built like Wolverine. She was mildly aware of the latter even as the impact sent her reeling, her breath stolen by the shock. He was so hard she'd have ricocheted into the wall behind her if he hadn't caught her with an arm that had to have been made of bedrock. The detail of his dark hair was lost to the dim light, but the same could not be said for his eyes. A striking ice-blue, their cool assessment left her skin pebbled, and her nipples wasted no time following suit, despite the ridiculous heat and rampant fear coiling through her.

Please let him be one of the good guys. He stood a head taller, an easy six foot something sexy, and was a little rough around the edges. As her eyes adjusted to the dark, she made out the beginnings of a five o'clock shadow that paired richly with chocolate-hued, bedroom-tussled hair. His hand slid along her forearm, his calloused fingers dragging out her inhibitions. *Oh, sweet Jesus.* He had the come hither glare down to a science, and she didn't think he was even trying.

"Can I help you find something?" he asked. His gaze again traveled the length of her body, lusciously slow. "Or someone?"

She swallowed. "I'm here for the Willie Focker affair."

At one time the wording had made her giggle. *You are cordially invited to experience an affair with Willie Focker.*

"That event is by invitation only. And generally accessible via the front door." A hint of bemusement tinged his otherwise firm words.

"I have an invitation," she said, though not as firmly as she would have liked. In such dim light, she had a hard time getting a read on the guy, which made her attraction to him all the more maddening.

In a voice as smooth as honey, he asked, "Would you like me to have someone escort you to the main entry?"

Disappointment frittered through her. *Not you?* But of course not. He likely had to keep his post to prevent people from sneaking in. Unauthorized versions of herself. "Look, my ticket fell into the toilet and was flushed away from me. Don't you have a list or something?"

He cocked a brow. "There's a list. At the front door. Which begs the question—if you're legit—of why you're sneaking in the back."

She hugged herself against a sudden chill. "Have you seen the mob in the hallway? I don't stand a chance out there."

He shook his head. "They're supposed to keep the door clear. If the group out there is anything like what Focker usually inspires, I don't blame you for not wanting to fight your way through. His groupies tend to be a bit...enthusiastic."

The final word ended with a wry upturn of his lips that left her flushed. She was one of those groupies, although looking at him made her wonder why. Focker was utterly perfect, at least as far as appearances went, but he had nothing on his bodyguard, whose tough guy exterior softened behind the play of a smile on his lips and the heated curiosity of his appraisal. Her earlier concerns about him being the bad guy eased. He didn't seem angry or tense, but amused. And not entirely at her expense, although she wasn't sure if sneaking in the back made her more or less manic than the screaming throng in the hall.

"You have any identification?" he asked.

Relief sluiced through her—before wariness set in. She may be from a small town, but she'd seen this all over Dateline. She would flash her identification, and he'd show up at her front door wielding a shovel and…a glass of wine. She could totally see him with wine. Wine and candlelight. He was way too sexy to be hiding in a dark room, and her body still singed from every single point of contact they'd shared. "How do I know you're not some predator?"

He flipped a light switch and held up the ID tag that hung from his neck on a lanyard. *Event staff.*

"That's a casino security badge," she said. Wariness edged back in. Was this guy back here hoping for the chance to seduce some desperate groupie? If so, he'd just struck out. "Do you even know Mr. Focker?"

Even in the dark, amusement glittered in his eyes. "As of three days ago, yes. I'm a local hired onto his detail for the RNC, but I can't move through this facility without a venue badge. Any guy on the street could make something up and flash it around if that were the case."

Oh.

She took a closer look at the badge, which he still withheld. *Jax Mathis.* She tried the name on her tongue, finding the silent utterance delicious. So much so that she couldn't help but wonder how the man himself would taste. Her best friend's pre-flight warning came back to her—something about how neon made people do crazy things. Only Ellie was pretty sure Taylor *wanted* her to do something crazy. There sure wasn't anything that qualified back home in Minturn, but there was no shortage of it in Vegas. And if what she were thinking about the man in front of her counted as crazy, she'd sure like to dip a toe in it now.

He stared her down, the dance of light in his eyes lending warmth to the most dizzying shade of blue she'd ever encountered. His muscles were a little less tense now, a little less on edge, but he still vibrated on an unfamiliar frequency. She stared at his arms and wondered what it would be like to be held by him.

His gaze promised to eat her alive. "What kind of predator do you think I am?" he asked.

"The kind that hangs out in dark rooms." She rubbed her arms, failing to eradicate the chill. "Waiting for prey."

An easy, bemused smile shaped his lips. "Well, I suppose I'm guilty of that, but if you're worried I'm going to show up in your room tonight, rest easy. I'm not above accompanying a beautiful woman back to her hotel, but not until she begs."

Until she begs. Not unless, but *until.* "Um, you said you could get me in to meet Mr. Focker."

"Identification?"

She withdrew her license and held it out for him, but not too close.

His brow lifted. "Colorado?"

"Actually, it's Ellie. Ellie Montgomery. I'm on the list."

He shrugged. "Which, again, I don't have."

She bit back a frustrated sigh. "Then why did you ask for my identification?"

"Because I wanted to know your name," he said, no trace of humor in his voice.

She tamped down the urge to throw something. He must have countless encounters with women every day, and he'd chosen *her* to give a hard time? Figured. Maybe if she pretended to lose it—not that she wasn't almost there any-way—he'd put those incredible arms around her. Frankly, she could use a little restraint, and it had increasingly little to with her desire to see what's-his-name. "There has to be a list. Can you ask the guy with the list?"

He grinned, all crooked and sexy. "Let me see if I have this right. Based on the way you came at me, I can only as-sume you're willing to risk jail time—*in Vegas*—to get close to this guy. Have you met him before?"

She shook her head, her thoughts still snagged on jail time. *In Vegas*. Good Lord, if the people roaming the streets made the cut for freedom, she could only imagine who hadn't.

"So how do you know he's not a complete ass?"

She didn't.

"Or gay?"

"I didn't come here to sleep with him."

"That's what they all say."

Oh, hell no. "I'm not them. I'm not…that. Not at all."

His eyes darkened. Did he believe her? Why did she care? "So educate me," he said. "What is it about meeting this guy that's worth time in the pen?"

"He's…" Words escaped her, primarily because the few that came to her applied not to Focker, but to the hard hunk of man challenging her. His tux, or maybe it was a suit, fit him like he'd had it tailored. Or sculpted. Or maybe that was just his body. What would a man like that feel like between her thighs? The ache that speared her at the thought would be only the beginning, of that she was sure.

"He's pretty," Jax supplied.

Sexiest man alive. But not the cover model. Not anymore.

Not next to Wolverine.

To his *pretty* assessment, she nodded, though the words rang as mockery. Rightfully so, at this point.

"Look," Jax said. "I can't let you in without a ticket, but I'll make you a deal. Let me take you out. Give me a chance to show you what a real man is like, and afterward if you still want to meet Pretty Boy I'll make personal introductions."

A real man. Had Wolverine really just asked her out? "You can do that?" Her mind flashed bedroom porn—her clutching sheets for dear life while he drove into her. The image, painfully brief, sent need tearing through her. She was in Las Vegas. Things like that totally happened here. Her clit happy-danced. She quaked. A little over the top, but considering the vision in her head, it was a miracle she hadn't dissolved entirely. "You can…introduce me to…?"

What the hell was his name?

"As we previously discussed," he said with a hint of humor, "I'm his bodyguard." He withdrew his wallet and presented his identification. Jax Mathis, take two. It matched the photo ID around his neck, but this version offered a Vegas address. "Google me. I'll wait."

Wariness forced some of the adrenaline from her veins, but the adrenaline pushed back. This was Vegas. If she couldn't do something crazy here, and with this man, she should probably just give up. Go home. Collect cats by the dozen—her mutt would just love that. Besides, a man who managed to look gorgeous in his driver's license photo was not to be trusted. That had to be a rule somewhere.

But what did that matter? This was Vegas. Rules didn't apply.

She swallowed her indecision, hoping courage would

somehow take its place. Rational thought edged through. "If you're his bodyguard, shouldn't you be...guarding him?"

"He's got security in there up to his eyeballs courtesy of the venue. They thought it was enough."

"And he didn't?"

His heated gaze scorched a trail down her body and back up again. "Was he wrong?"

She shot him her best death glare, but he didn't flinch. Instead, he smiled. It was pure devastation, and not because he was keeping her from her cover model. "So what's it going to be?" he asked. "Me or hotel security?"

"That's blackmail."

"I prefer to think of it as a reprieve. Time off for good behavior—or bad, if that's your preference."

His tone—the suggestion in his words—made her thighs quake. It took all of two seconds to find her phone in the teeny little handbag that had sent her ticket to swim with the fishes. *Jax Mathis*. Thirty seconds later, she had reasonable proof the man in front of her was legit.

He cocked an eyebrow. "Well?"

"I have a better idea."

"What's that?" he asked, humor threading his tone.

"You take me in to meet Mr. Focker."

He shook his head. One of those *I-don't-believe-this* gestures that suggested she was crazy. Maybe so, but she might as well own it.

"And this differs from your original plan *how*?" he asked.

"You think you're the better man, so prove it. Introduce us. Let me decide." She met that hard blue gaze with all the nerve she could muster—nerve that had nothing to do with meeting Focker and everything to do with the heat emanating off his bodyguard—and treated him to her most innocent smile.

A corner of his mouth tipped. He invaded her space just a little, and her body begged for her to throw the white flag of surrender, to fall against that wall of man and find out if he was hard all over. Everywhere but his lips…they appeared soft. Sensual. And they oh-so-sensually curved into a smile.

"Suppose I agree to this," he said, his voice husky with bedroom tones. Blue eyes devoured her, and in that moment she desperately wanted his lips to do the same. Her breathing grew shallow with anticipation and nearly stopped when he toyed with the tips of her hair, tugging gently. When his fingertips traced her spine, she bit back a gasp. Her eyes fluttered closed before she could make the effort to stop them. When he spoke, his deep voice rumbled dangerously close to her ear. "What happens when you realize I'm right?"

With him that close, she couldn't see straight, much less string together syllables. "Right…about…what?"

A grin touched his lips, his words tearing through her. "He may be pretty, Colorado, but are his hands rough? Can he work them inside you until your knees give out? Until you can't breathe?" He let the suggestions hover. Wreck her. "When you lie in your bed tonight, wanting someone to touch you, are you going to think about him posing on the front of a damned book cover, or are you going to think of me?"

Oh, dear God. Would she ever *stop* thinking of Jax? Was that even an option? And what the hell was happening here? Desire devoured her. She was dizzy. She didn't need to give a second's consideration to answer his question. There was only one answer, and he knew it. "You."

She expected triumph to shape his face, but it didn't. If anything, he turned more serious. Ice blue eyes regarded her, their intensity deepening. His hand rested lightly on her back. Too lightly. She wanted him to haul her against him, to make good on any one of those promises. To teach her firsthand what those undoubtedly talented fingers could do.

But not yet.

"I'll be thinking of you," she repeated, a little stronger this time. "But if you don't let me meet Willie Focker, I won't be thinking of what you can do with your fingers, but where I want to put my foot." She grinned as his faded.

"Put your money where your mouth is, Jax Mathis. If you're a real man, prove it."

Chapter Two

Well, hot damn. Jax suppressed a grin. The sexy little wildcat had claws, and they were hot as hell paired with that tight black dress. He shouldn't have tried to blackmail her, as she put it, but any guilt he might have felt had been eradicated the moment she handed him that challenge.

Out man Focker? No problem. Having been hired specifically for the Vegas convention, Jax had only known the guy a couple of days, but he wasn't hard to read. The dude might be pretty, but he didn't have a manly bone in his body. Focker wouldn't open his own car door because he worried he'd wreck his manicure. He demanded someone carry an umbrella to shelter him and his precious skin from the desert sun. He had facials nightly. He also claimed he had all the sex he wanted, and no doubt he did, but Jax would bet money it wasn't the hot, sweaty, down and dirty kind.

Looking at Ellie, he couldn't imagine anything less.

"I think that sounds like blackmail, Colorado." Ironic

that he'd call her out, seeing as how she'd done nothing more than turn the tables on him. But he could make a night out of giving her a hard time. In fact, he planned on it.

"Take it or leave it," she said, as feisty and stubborn as she was beautiful.

"I think that was my line."

"Operative word being *was*," she shot back.

He couldn't help the grin that reshaped his mouth. He'd never forgive himself if she were playing him, but it didn't matter. Making demands of a woman who didn't want to give in wasn't his thing. But convincing this one to give him a shot? Most definitely a thing.

In lieu of answering her, he snagged his phone from his pocket and called hotel security. When he requested someone come take his place at the so-called back door, Ellie flashed a victorious grin that weakened his knees but had the exact opposite effect on his dick.

"I win?" she asked.

He leaned down until his lips grazed her ear. "No, darlin'. I do."

Her eyes widened, but he didn't stick around long enough to get lost in them. His pants were already uncomfortably tight in ways that had nothing to do with being forced into a damned tux. He'd give anything for jeans and a t-shirt right about then—especially if a certain gorgeous brunette might be interested in stripping them off. He hoped he hadn't imagined the spark of interest in her eyes. He was no Focker, but Jax would put that in the pro column any day of the week. Hopefully she'd come to the same conclusion when she met the airhead cover model.

He tugged at his collar as he left the room, the clack

of Ellie's heels suggesting she was right behind him. Hotel security passed him in the hall, confirming the door would be covered. Good enough. Jax rounded the corner and came to a stop. No fewer than twenty women stood in the hall screaming Focker's name.

Business as usual.

Jax reached for Ellie's hand. Without thinking, he laced his fingers through hers—way more intimate than necessary when a simple lobster claw would have sufficed—and edged his way through the throng, tugging her in his wake. At his intrusion, the women momentarily fell silent, but as soon as security opened the door for him, all hell broke loose. He quickly ushered Ellie ahead of him, living a full lifetime in the moments that sweet ass of hers spent pressed to the front of his pants as he urged her along. By the time the door closed behind them, it was he who stood dumbstruck while she laid eyes on her hero for the first time.

Focker stood shirtless near his life size cardboard romance book cover, women flanking him on both sides. He flashed his toothpaste commercial smile at each of them in turn, just like his manager told him. *Make every woman feel like the only one in the room.* Fine for professional reasons, but Jax didn't like it. If he told a woman she was beautiful, it was because he meant it. Not because he wanted to sell another book with his face on it. Focker, who thought himself the Fabio of his generation, was vain even by Vegas standards, and that was saying something. Too bad he didn't have a personality to go along with it. The man was about as entertaining as a brick, but that sure didn't keep the women from screaming his name.

The guy at the door charged with checking identification

was hard-eyeing him, so Jax left Ellie to her gawking and went to check her in. He hoped her story checked out and she was really on that list. If not, he could just name her as his plus one, but he didn't want to go out later with someone who had lied to his face. And he definitely wanted to see her again. Body contact was all over his to-do list.

"Ellie Montgomery," he told the guy with the list.

He marked something on his tablet. "You check her ID?"

Jax nodded. "Before I let her through the door."

"Good deal. That makes a full house. Maybe we can seal that door, so to speak, and the crowd will dissipate." Door check guy's tone suggested he didn't think it likely.

Jax agreed. He hadn't needed days to understand the hype around Focker. He'd discovered that before they'd been formally introduced, while he was part of the detail trying to get the cover model from the car to his hotel room. Three in the morning and they'd been mobbed on the sidewalk like he was a fucking rock star. Hotel security had cut off the flow in the lobby, but the screams still rang in Jax's ears long after the elevator doors slid shut. "Something, isn't it?"

Door check guy nodded. "Yeah. If I wanted to work the shows, I would have. I never figured the conference rooms would be so...shrill."

Jax glanced in the direction of Focker, where he expected he'd find the women. But one hung back. Ellie wasn't far from where he'd left her, and rather than drooling over Focker, she watched Jax. And she wasn't shy about it, either. When his eyes locked onto hers, her mouth slipped into an easy smile that made him want to tear up the distance between them and taste those full, lush lips. He'd give any-thing to see her lashes flutter closed under the promise of a kiss. To feel those curves pressed against him again. She had him twisted inside out, and he wasn't sure why. Something about that fresh-faced innocence demanded he pay atten-tion, and those long, gorgeous legs and that spectacular ass made it nonnegotiable.

"Don't let Focker see you've upstaged him," list guy said.

Jax blinked, his mind still caught on replaying the shudder that went through Ellie when he mentioned sex. "What?"

"That one only has eyes for you. If Focker notices, he'll lose his shit."

Jax grinned. "In theory. But what are the odds of him noticing anyone other than himself?"

The joke landed a little too close to the truth. "I see first impressions are more than skin deep."

A pang of guilt assaulted Jax. Granted, he didn't par-ticularly like Focker, but his contract had been more than fair and his ego, while inflated, had certainly gotten that way honestly. Jax hadn't seen that many screaming women since he'd had to guard the stage door to one of those boy band concerts. Bottom line, Focker did his thing and his fans re-sponded. Damned hard to fault a man for that. "Nah, he's a good guy. His entourage seems to love him. He just rolls on a different frequency like most of the celebrities who blow through here."

"Looks like he's noticed your girl."

Jax watched, an unfamiliar feeling curling through his gut when Focker set his sights on Ellie. The fact that she didn't stand in line to fawn over him probably made her more interesting than every other woman in the room, and Jax didn't like where that could lead. "Excuse me."

He walked over to Ellie before Focker—who had been stopped by yet another fan—could get to her. Jax nodded in Focker's direction. "Shall we?" he asked.

"Shall we what?"

"I owe you a personal introduction," he said gruffly.

She stared at him, confusion touching her eyes. No shocker there…Jax had a sudden grudge about his boss that hadn't been there before, and it came through in his tone. "You got me in," she said. "That's enough."

"No, it's not." Especially not now that Focker had noticed her. Jax had no right to stake a claim on Ellie, but he had a feeling Focker had taken one look at all that untapped innocence and was already making plans to haul her upstairs. Jax couldn't keep that from happening, but it sure as hell wouldn't happen in front of him.

He took her hand—again with the damned hand—and led her to Focker. His security badge worked wonders…once the women immediately surrounding the model noticed Jax, they actually parted the waters a little. It wouldn't have happened if not for the intimate setting, he was sure. Here, they were all guaranteed a moment with their hero.

Focker greeted Ellie with his stage smile. Jax supposed he thought it charming. Whatever. He tried not to glare at Focker as he broke every rule of etiquette by presenting Focker to Ellie rather than the other way around. Focker would probably never know the difference, but he wasn't the important one to Jax. Ellie was.

"Ellie Montgomery, I'd like you to meet Willie Focker." Jax would never get used to that stupid name. It couldn't be on the guy's birth certificate. If it was, he had either the worst parents ever...or the coolest. "Mr. Focker, Ellie Montgomery."

Focker took Ellie's hand and pressed it to his lips.

Jax prepared for the meltdown women tended to have in Focker's presence, but it didn't happen. Neither did any sparkling conversation.

"You look lovely, Ellie," Focker said. "Thank you for joining me this evening."

Lovely? Jax cringed over the obviously canned greeting.

"It's my honor," she said. Politely, but with a gush factor of zero.

"Ellie's here from Colorado," Jax supplied.

Focker's canned smile got a little brighter. "An international guest?"

Ellie cut her eyes at Jax. "No, the state. Near Denver."

The cover model straightened, like the flub had pumped him up. *Idiot.* "Well, it's great you were able to attend," Focker said. "What made you enter the contest?"

Jax braced himself for the Focker-is-God spiel.

It didn't come.

"I found the card in a book and sent it in on a whim." She shrugged. "I never thought I'd win, but any excuse to go to Vegas, right?"

Focker blinked with confusion. "Right. But you're a fan of mine?"

"I have quite a few books with you on the cover, but I think you're on the cover of almost all of them, aren't you?" She smiled sweetly.

Jax wondered if not a bit *too* sweetly, but he kept his mouth shut. No way he'd call her out on failing to drool over the guy.

"Almost." Focker laid on another one of those T-Rex grins. "But my collection wouldn't be complete without you in it. Care to join me for a photo?"

Damned if she didn't hesitate, her gaze darting to Jax's. He nudged her. "Give me your phone, and I'll take a few candids for you to go with the final shot." He figured she'd want the evidence as soon as possible, whereas the professional shots would be edited and approved by Focker's team before they were sent to each guest's home address — a process that would take days, if not weeks.

Ellie extracted her phone from her purse, opened the lock screen, then handed him both items. She laughed. "Goes great with your outfit."

He stood there, slightly dumbstruck to be holding a little sparkly purse. Then he realized Focker had his arm around her and the odd feeling in his gut flared. Jax wasn't one of those *mine at first sight* types. He avoided attachments, which was easy enough to do in a place where the majority of the population came and went with the rising sun. He didn't have time for the empty ones, and he didn't deserve anything real — not after what he'd done. What he'd *lost*. But despite the shadows of regret he'd never before been able to shake, he wanted to get to know Ellie. The urge was as foreign as her sparkly purse and no less out of place.

Focker's handlers were getting him and Ellie in position in front of the life size book cover that boasted a background flush with draped fabric and the title *Bedded for Her Pleasure*.

Nothing like an ego, that was for damned sure.

Ellie, with her hair falling in shiny waves and her little

black dress clinging to every curve, looked the part of the heroine, but she didn't belong in Focker's arms. Jax didn't like her there. He didn't know what that meant, but there it was. Feral emotion tore him up inside. And he was documenting every moment.

Holding a purse.

After an interminable period of time that couldn't have in reality spanned more than ten minutes, they wrapped up their shoot. Ellie escaped Focker's clutches flushed and laughing. Fucking gorgeous.

Ellie stepped away from Focker, but she didn't get far before he put a hand on her arm.

"Would you like to join me for drinks after the event?" he asked her.

Jax felt like he'd been punched. Ellie said she wasn't there to sleep with Focker, but *join me for drinks* was code for *get fucked solid,* and Jax had a feeling he'd be the one facing jail time if Ellie said yes. Which was pretty much ridiculous considering they'd just met, but it was fact all the same.

Jax invaded their solitude and handed her the purse and phone. He started to step away, but Ellie tucked her arm in his.

"Thank you for the offer," she said to Focker. "I can't tell you how much of an honor it is that you've asked, but as it turns out I have plans."

The shock that splayed across Focker's face was almost funny. Almost. Jax had known the man all of two days, and he'd seen him ask no fewer than ten women to have so-called drinks. His offer had never been met with an ounce of hesitance, let alone a flat-out rejection.

"You have plans?" Focker asked, a trace of sheet-white marring his perfect spray tan.

"I sure do." She glanced at Jax. "Turns out I have a date with a hero of my own."

. . .

Ellie twirled her straw in her drink and flashed a smile that put the sun to shame, not that Jax ever saw anything celestial through Vegas's neon lights. She managed to pack the gesture with enough sincerity and self-deprecation that he wondered if his judgment had gone to hell. Every other woman he'd had to peel off Focker's tail had lost her shit when he'd come between her and her perceived destiny. This one had turned down a private meeting with Focker in favor of a date with Jax.

He wasn't sure how he felt about that.

"I'm not usually like this," she said.

"Like what?" *Drop dead gorgeous?* Beautiful women were a dime a dozen in Vegas. No reason this one should have caught his attention, but when he'd seen her get that look in her eyes over Focker something primal had torn through Jax's gut. Pretty Boy Focker had a new way to get his dick wet every night of the week, and the way he talked, no one had yet to complain about a one-night rodeo, even if it was probably vanilla as hell so Focker didn't risk a ding to his perfect appearance. But Ellie...Ellie looked like she believed in something. Jax didn't know what, but he didn't want her to turn those trusting eyes on a man guaranteed to break her heart. It wasn't until her honey brown irises rested on Jax that he remembered he was no upgrade. He had more baggage than a carousel at McCarran, and that was putting it lightly.

She traced the rim of her glass with a glossed fingernail. Not a fancy manicure, he noted. In fact, she wasn't the usual painted type at all. She had a natural beauty that put the overdone showgirls and their pasties to shame. "I don't have a habit of trying to sneak into places," she said. "Or getting picked up by strangers who threaten to have me arrested. Or having dinner after eleven."

Pushing midnight or not, the Masquerade's Topenga was hopping. The buffet had closed for the day, but the place served up burgers and fries all night long. He would have preferred a smaller restaurant away from the main drag, but he didn't want to take her off grid. The crowds and the lights and the casino noises provided a nice buffer between her and whatever predatory measures she thought he had in mind. If that helped her relax, he was all for it.

But if she thought eleven was late, she'd better think again.

He leaned in and crossed one tattooed arm over the other on the table. "Welcome to Vegas, where you're not doing it right if you're in bed before the sun comes up."

She graced him with a flirtatious grin. "Does that mean I have a long night ahead?"

Oh, hell yes. But it wasn't nice to scare the tourists. "Colorado, if you think it's a long night then I'm not holding up my end of the bargain."

She blushed, all pretty and sweet. The kind of innocent that had no place in Sin City, let alone a table width from him. He'd corrupt the hell out of her, given half the chance, but he'd hate to think he'd steal the sunshine from her eyes.

What the fuck are you doing? He never should have started this thing. The last time he'd cared about someone, she'd ended up dead. There was no way he was going there again…not even for the first woman in a long time who'd lit a fire to something more than his arousal.

Ellie squirmed a little, and he realized he'd been dragging his gaze over her a little too recklessly. A little too long. "What do you do back home?" he asked.

"I'm a ski instructor in Vail."

Jesus Christ. No wonder she had such gorgeous legs. There was something beautiful about a woman who got her curves the natural way. Conquering the leg machine at the gym had nothing on conquering a mountain, but the irony was a bitter pill. He knew the mountains. Had left them for a damned good reason—one that still hurt after sixteen years.

He picked up a fry and dragged it through ketchup, fighting for neutrality in his voice. "What about the offseason?"

"I freelance for the ski mags and volunteer at the local hospital. What do you do when you're not…guarding bodies?"

"I hit the desert." Not the mountains. At least not the ones like hers.

She smiled. "Chasing adrenaline?"

Protest stopped in his throat. She didn't need to know he was out there searching for salvation. Forgiveness. Anything to ease the shitstorm that ate at him. *Anything* but getting high on adrenaline, that was for damn sure.

"Is that what you do out there?" He kept his tone neutral. "Chase adrenaline?"

"Nope."

He looked up in surprise. "Those mountains you climb

suggest otherwise."

"I wouldn't exactly call riding a chair lift *climbing*."

He raised his brow. "I stand corrected. Those mountains you ski say otherwise."

She pushed back a loose strand of hair. Her eyes sparkled with excitement. "I know this sounds weird, but I didn't fall in love with the mountains for the thrill. It's the solitude. It's humbling. It's a gift, in a way, to stand there in all that grandeur and be a part of it. It's raw, but it's pure. Kind of primal, but in a beautiful, back to nature kind of way."

He'd give her *primal*...right after he got the hell off the floor. Her reasons for tearing through the mile-high Rockies with fiberglass blades strapped to her feet were exactly his for wandering aimlessly through the desert. Granted, she chose the path of exhilaration, but she got him. She fucking *got him*.

"Why did you say yes to me?" The question—or perhaps her answer—carried an importance he didn't care to examine.

She looked at her drink and started stirring the hell out of it. "Might have been the ultimatum."

He reached out and closed his hand over hers, ceasing her motion. "That wasn't it."

Her eyes had a little brush with panic, and he almost felt bad. But almost didn't cut it.

"Come on, Colorado. There had to be a reason."

She shrugged. Tried to play it off with a nervous smile. "You know what they say about Vegas."

He choked back a humorless laugh. "I know good little girls don't give a damn what they say about Vegas."

"Well, I guess it's convenient I'm not here on good

behavior."

His hand still covered hers, so he knew she practically shook with the effort to spit out the words. But it didn't matter. Sweet little Ellie Montgomery from Colorado had given him a chance.

The jury was still out on whether he was dumb enough to take it.

Chapter Three

Ellie figured the Masquerade Hotel and Casino was a stand-out, even for Vegas. If New Orleans and an Anywhere, USA amusement park carousel had a baby, the Masquerade, in all of its striped pole and beaded glory, would be it. The façade would have been gaudy absolutely anywhere else in the world, but somehow the flags and enormous colored balls were right at home on the effusive Vegas strip.

She turned a circle on the sidewalk, which might have been more crowded with people after one in the morning than it had been at the more reasonable hour of sixish when her taxi eased down the strip en route from the airport. Traffic was surprisingly light, even at the earlier hour, but cabs were plentiful, and she imagined designated drivers were few and far between. Designated *walkers*, on the other hand, weren't a thing at all. One such reveler compounded his gravity problem with a loud, terribly off-key rendition of "Let it Go" to a companion whose expression indicated she had no such intention. In his voracity, he threw out his arms, lost his balance, and almost took down Ellie despite the berth she'd given him.

But Jax was there. He made an effortless one arm save that drew her tight against his body and left her breathless in a way that had nothing to do with the near miss. Could he *be* more gorgeous? He'd shed the formal wear in favor of jeans and a T-shirt, the latter in a soft blue that made his eyes lethal in their intensity. Looking up at them now, it was no wonder he'd been collecting appreciative glances like they were dropped casino chips.

"Thanks," she muttered. But in her head, it sounded more like *don't let go*. The man was *ermahgerd* hot, and while she'd always preferred her mile-high existence in the Rocky Mountains, there was definitely something to be said for what the Nevada desert had to offer. She couldn't forget what he'd said to her, nor could she shake the thrilling promise of his words. No man had ever spoken to her in such a way. Before Jax, she would have said it would be a total turnoff, but now she craved more.

"Are you sure you want to walk the strip?" he asked with a quiet laugh.

Right after you show me what those fingers can do. But she didn't dare say it. Despite her absolute craving for Jax, she really didn't do casual sex...yet she couldn't be more tempted. It had to be Vegas. Excitement and energy thrummed from every neon pore of the city and made her feel alive. Reckless. "Yep," she said of the walk. "It was the first thing I wanted to do when I got here, but I figured I wouldn't get the chance."

He raised his brow and gave her a curious, if amused,

look. "I thought Pretty Boy was the first thing you wanted to do when you got here."

She flushed hot and fervently prayed he'd chalk it up to the neon ambiance. Ignoring his statement — and the evidence to the contrary, seeing as how she'd turned down Mr. Focker's invitation for a private party — she said, "I didn't think it would be a good idea to walk alone at night, but I see *alone* isn't a thing here."

Jax had barely eased his rescue grip. "Alone is definitely a thing here," he said, "but there are always plenty of witnesses to it."

She forced herself to take a step back. *Oxygen.* There had to be oxygen somewhere out of his orbit, but heaven only knew how far that extended. She hadn't been able to take her eyes off of him all night. It almost irritated her that her years of adoring her book hero had culminated in her standing there feeling awkward while he held her for the book cover photo op. Rather than melting in his arms, she was focused on Jax. Wanting to get back to him. Hoping he meant what he said about taking her out. He'd been right about Focker. The man seemed nice enough, but his fingernails were prettier than hers, and he apparently didn't know Colorado was part of the United States. Two turnoffs too many.

Jax took a sideways step to avoid a group of women with legs down to *there* and dresses up to *here.* To his credit, he didn't so much as glance their way. The lump in her throat festered.

Wolverine likes you.

In dodging the women, he closed that little bit of distance between she and Jax, but instead of standing there stealing air, he turned and in one smooth motion managed to snag her hand and lead her through a crowd waiting for a bus. Her heart stuttered at the gesture. Five seconds in, she'd bet her palm was soaked and with his fingers laced through hers, he probably felt every drop.

"Is this crowd every night?" she asked. "Or is this a Thursday thing?"

"There's not a Thursday thing," he said. "Not on this section of the boulevard."

"Not because of the convention?"

"The convention is a drop in the bucket." He gestured to the wall of lights that stretched from the Stratosphere to Mandalay Bay. "Figure there are over a hundred and twenty thousand hotel rooms, then throw in some double occupancy and a bachelor party or ten, and you've got business as usual."

"On a Thursday?" she squeaked. Though they now had their pocket of sidewalk to themselves, he still held her hand.

He laughed. "People don't come here to care what day it is. I take it you've never been here before?"

"No. Never wanted to."

"Well, in that case I guess I owe Pretty Boy a cold one."

So did she, but try as she might she couldn't seem to remember the face that graced almost every romance novel she owned. Jax would probably have that effect on anyone, but the concession didn't stop guilt from tapping at her conscience. If Jax had been on a book cover next to Focker, she'd have chosen Jax, hands down. She wanted to tell him as much, but to her own mind the confession sounded more like backpedaling than sincerity. It wasn't enough in her own mind that she'd chosen Jax. His words had rocked her to the core. The truth of that scared her as much as it intrigued her, but the bottom line was the same: she wanted more. She wanted *him*. But now that they were away from the closely guarded Focker affair, she was a little nervous. A little shy.

"You know a lot about the city," she said instead.

"It's part of the job."

She blinked. "Keeping a running count of the number of hotel rooms is part of the job?"

"Not exactly," he said, "but knowing my surroundings is. Vegas lends itself to statistics. People like to memorize every random detail. I guess they feel less like they'll lose their shirts that way."

"What about you?" she asked. "You ever lose your shirt?"

He dragged his free hand across his abdomen, showing off the promise of washboard abs, and grinned. "Not anywhere I couldn't find it again later."

Something in his tone absolutely suggested sex. Either that, or her mind had gone straight to the gutter, which wasn't a hard sell considering the number of sex ads they'd passed in a single block.

She forced away unbidden images of Jax with his perfect body sweaty and tangled in sheets. *Her* sheets. "So you just memorize facts?"

"Nah. I have a good memory, and working security isn't always the most entertaining job so I tend to read whatever's handy. On the floor, I have to stay alert. But guarding a door on the off chance someone beautiful will surprise me gives me some down time."

Yeah, that was her again, but...*beautiful*? She shivered, and his grip on her hand tightened. "Why does Will—Mr. Focker need a bodyguard?"

"You mean besides all those screaming women?"

Her face heated…again. "Yeah, besides that."

"He's had some pretty specific threats for this event. So-cial media makes it a little too easy to get to someone, so we have no way of knowing if they're credible or just some husband sitting at home pissed off that his wife is here soak-ing her panties over some other guy."

"So you take it seriously until you know otherwise?"

"Exactly. Only you never really know otherwise. Could be a prank or a genuine threat from someone who lost the balls to follow through."

She grimaced at his candor. "Which is a good thing."

"Yeah, that's a good thing."

His so-called good thing still sounded terrifying. "Does your family worry about you doing this job? Is it like secret service, where you're supposed to take the bullet first?"

His eyes darkened, but his tone remained casual. "I'd fling myself on the attacker before the bullet, but yeah, there's less of a guarantee that I'll see tomorrow than the next guy."

"Your mother must be sick." Ellie was, and she didn't even know Jax.

"If she is," he said, "it's not over me. She hasn't spoken to me in a long time. Neither has my father."

Ouch. And yet she forged on. "Do you have any siblings?"

Did a shadow cross his face, or was it the play of neon? It was hard to tell, especially in a place that was the visual equivalent of being inside a pinball machine. "One. A sister."

"Does she live here?"

"Nope." The flat, one-word answer should have told her to leave it alone, but she didn't.

"Do you talk to her?" Ellie persisted.

"Every goddamn day," he bit out.

Alrighty then. Shadows not imagined. "Do you get along?"

He crammed his hand in his pocket. A muscle in his jaw flexed. "We did until she died."

The blunt truth cut right through her. "Oh, no, I'm so sorry."

"It's been a few years," he said, more wistful now. "I still miss her. I talk to her to keep her close. I don't want to... forget."

Ellie blinked back unexpected emotion. That a big, tough guy like Jax would do something so sweet and sentimental set her back a few notches. Suddenly all the physical attraction edged into new territory.

"Have you ever played the slots?" he asked.

The sudden change of subject came with a forced-sounding lighter tone. She took it. "Never."

He led her into the nearest doorway. Like every other one they passed, it led to a football-field-sized room lit almost entirely by slot machines, approximately half of which were occupied.

After one in the morning. On a Thursday. Or Friday. Whatever.

He pulled a couple of singles from his pocket and fed the nearest machine, then gestured for her to sit. *Eight credits,* the machine read. "Where's the handle?" she asked.

"Back in the nineteen nineties," he said. "There are a few old school coin slots around somewhere, I'm sure, but most everything is computerized now."

"Can't they, I don't know, tell the computer not to let

you win?"

"Not if they don't want to be shut down. There's a minimum required payout per machine. Slots aren't the best way to make a killing, and ultimately the house always wins, but it's not rigged so you can't walk away with a few bucks." He leaned down over her shoulder. His scent encompassed her like a cloak. Or a duvet. She could crawl beneath one of those any minute now, especially if it smelled like him. Pointing, he said, "Those are your credits. Quarter slot, two bucks, so eight credits. You choose how many credits to play, then hit the button."

She studied the machine. It looked a lot more complicated than he made it out to be. "How many credits should I play?"

"Any number you want, but the more credits you play, the faster the money is gone."

"So I just hit this button?" When he nodded, she pressed the blinking light and set the pictures in motion. When they stopped, she was down to seven credits. "That was surprisingly undramatic," she said.

"Try it again." His voice reverberated so close to her ear that she felt it to her toes. She didn't really care when she ended up another credit down. Then another. When the machine flashed on her fourth spin, she thought it must have been her overloaded senses screaming jackpot over the man who practically had his arms around her, but then the man in question pointed to her number of credits.

"You're up to a hundred and twenty four," he explained.

She turned her head only to lose her breath when she found he was even closer than she'd thought. "What does that mean?"

He tipped his head just enough to make her anticipate a kiss that didn't come. Instead, he offered a boyish grin that had her thinking of very adult things. "You just won about thirty bucks," he said. "Which means if you stop now, you'll have achieved the impossible."

"What's that?"

"First time gambling, you won Vegas."

God, the man melted her. But he was wrong. "Not quite."

The corner of his mouth quirked. "What do you mean?"

"My first win wasn't here," she said. "It was back at the Masquerade. Door number two."

Chapter Four

Jax could only stare as Ellie's words sank in. Jesus, this woman. All he'd wanted was to keep her away from Focker. Jerk move for all the right reasons, and now Jax was paying with his soul. He wasn't so bothered by the fact that he wanted to taste her every delectable inch, but that he was already picturing the morning after. Pancakes in bed. Licking syrup from her nipples. Wrecked sheets and sex. Wrecked *him*. And it was too damned much, especially considering his number one rule was to never spend the night. He'd found out the hard way that waking up next to the same woman he'd gone to bed with triggered something in her that said *relationship*, and it was a mistake he wouldn't make twice.

Getting personal — letting someone believe in him — was a mistake he'd never make again.

One funeral had been enough.

"Let's cash out," Ellie said, oblivious to his dark thoughts. "My friend back home gave me enough grief for coming here. She said I'd never loosen up enough to have any fun so I want at least one winning ticket to show her."

"Then you better take a picture of it." He showed her how to print the voucher, then used her phone to take a picture of her holding the slip for her friend. "That okay?" he asked, holding up the picture for her approval.

She peered at the image, then at him. "Almost. Do you mind being in the picture with me?"

Oh, hell. The lowest of lows…a selfie with a cash out ticket. He'd have to turn in his right to call himself a local if he agreed. He did it anyway, just in case Ellie ever wanted to look back and remember him. Another dumb move for a guy who generally preferred to be forgotten, but at some point the rules had left the building.

She snapped the picture then showed him. And it cut like a knife.

We look like a couple.

Worse, he liked it. He *liked* looking like he belonged with someone. Liked looking like he belonged with *her.*

Hated the sudden urge he had to ask her to send him a copy.

"Evidence preserved," she said with a grin. "Now how do we cash out?"

"Kiosk." He pointed toward one of the ATM-like stations that traded vouchers for cash and waited off to one side while the machine paid out. As he stood there, he scoped out his surroundings, and in particular the people. Very much in particular the jerk standing way too close to Ellie. He hadn't quit staring at her butt since he'd had the good fortune of getting in line behind her. Jax could hardly blame the guy. The woman quite possibly had the tightest ass he'd ever seen, and the snug fit of her pants didn't let him forget it.

When she turned toward him, she walked so close he wondered if he was about to get the most amazing kiss of his life. Instead, she discretely pressed cash into his hand. "I think this is yours."

He needed a moment to remember he'd funded her slot machine adventure. Once that hit him, he countered by closing his hand over hers. "No way, Colorado. That was on me."

She looked up at him, all sweetness and *pretty please*. "Will you at least let me give back the two dollars?"

"Tomorrow," he promised.

"Tomorrow?"

"Yes." Despite lingering thoughts over losing his sister, he didn't have to force the smile Ellie brought to his face. "If you let me see you again tomorrow."

She offered a wicked little grin that belied all that wholesome innocence that, at least in his mind, belonged to her. "What if I'm not finished seeing you tonight?" she asked.

Oh, hell yes. Rather than attempt to form words in response to what sounded a heck of a lot like an invitation, he pulled her into an alcove along the wall. Once he had her semi-alone, he wound his fingers through her hair, capturing the back of her head and leaning down to meet her.

"You sure about that, Colorado?"

She nodded, her attention pegged on his mouth. Her breathing was quick, her lips parted, and he wanted nothing more than to claim them for his own.

"I want to kiss you so damned bad," he said. "I want to know if those lips are anywhere near as soft as they look. I want to feel firsthand how your body responds to me." With his lips grazing her ear, he added, "*I want to drench you.*"

Her sharp intake of breath sent the last of his blood to his dick. God, he wanted her. She looked up at him through drowsy, hooded eyes, no apparent clue that they were still in view of the public. The electronic dings and noises of the casino faded to the background, and he thought long and hard about kissing her. But he didn't want to be the guy like any other she might know. He wanted to be the man she'd never forget.

With his fingers wound through her hair, he could think of little more than driving into her. Fucking her hard while she made little good girl whimpers that were lost to deep, consuming kisses. He wanted to possess her. To be possessed.

"Then do it," she said. So softly he wasn't sure he heard. "Drench me."

He froze. Then ever so slowly he descended to touch his mouth to the pulse point on her neck. The warmth of her skin dizzied him. Her moan when his lips pressed against her flesh nearly did him in.

His phone chose that very moment to ring, and it was Focker's ring tone. That *dick*. "Son of a…I need to answer this."

She nodded, a little slow to follow him out of the alcove. She didn't further follow him, though, when he edged a few feet away to dodge the bulk of the casino noise. "Mathis."

"I'm having a private party," Focker said. "I need you up here just in case."

Jax shook his head. Leave it to Focker to invite people to his room when he didn't fucking trust them. He didn't blame the dude for being paranoid—he'd gotten several threats that he'd be leaving Vegas in a body bag—but it was pushing two in the morning and Focker was partial to his beauty sleep. "Don't you have an event in the morning?"

"I'm *trying* to have an event tonight."

Jax rolled his eyes. "I'll be there in thirty."

"Make it fifteen."

"I'm not in the hotel," Jax explained. "You're going to have to settle for thirty."

"I'll settle for fifteen," Focker said, and hung up.

Jax shook his head. He had no idea what Ellie saw in the pompous little jerk, but it didn't matter. He had her...for now. And maybe that was Focker's problem.

She approached when he slid the phone in his pocket. "Anything wrong?"

"Nothing's wrong, but duty calls." Inconvenient as it was, at least the conundrum of how the night would end was settled. He felt like a kid on his first date, all unsure if Ellie wanted him to kiss her or shake her hand or take her to her room and fuck her senseless. He was all for the third option, but mentioning it might be impolite.

He took her hand, earning another brilliant smile that consumed him. He was a better man for it.

The walk back to the Masquerade passed far too quickly, the night ending on someone else's terms when Focker's manager met him in the lobby. And Ellie, just like she had when he'd gotten the phone call, immediately gave him space.

Only he didn't want it.

Before he could get her number—phone, room, anything—she'd disappeared behind the elevator doors. Focker's manager—who should have been with the cover model if it was such an emergency—practically had Jax by the scruff.

Jax brushed him off. Hard. "What the fuck, man?"

"He got another threatening text. Party is canceled. He wants you posted outside his door until he leaves for his first event in the morning."

Jax stared at the long-closed elevator doors that had swallowed Ellie. Screw this. He didn't have her room number. Or her phone number. And now this crap with Focker. "He got a text in the last ten minutes?"

"Right after he called you."

Great. Jax would be a zombie by morning if he didn't get any sleep. He was already twenty hours in without so much as a nap, though it hadn't hit him until she had left him. "Give me a minute with the front desk to track down a guest."

"I don't think you should make him wait."

Jax took a steadying breath in an attempt not to lose it on the manager. "Tell him it's someone who tried to sneak in to the meet and greet earlier."

Focker's manager grunted. "Did you report that?"

"No, I handled it. Which is what I'm being paid to do, but I can't be on twenty-four-hour shifts. Tell Focker I'm on my way, but I have tomorrow off."

"He won't like that."

"He doesn't have to like it," Jax said. It was a fight to keep his tone even, but losing it would get him booted from a very well-paying job and would leave Focker down a man. That wouldn't bode any better for Jax's career than it would his conscience, but some things were nonnegotiable. "I'm no good to him if I'm falling asleep. We have a contract and he's already fucking with it."

"Fine. I'll deal with him. You've got five minutes."

That was all he needed. Jax made a beeline for the front desk. "I need a room number for a guest."

The kid behind the counter stared through pried-open eyes. Must be new to third shift. "I'm sorry, sir. That's against our policy."

Maybe not so new after all. Jax withdrew a wad of cash. "Is it still against your policy?"

The guy perked. "Perhaps I can send the guest in question a message?"

"Yes, do that." Jax crammed the money back in his pocket. He happened to know messages *were* hotel policy, and therefore free.

Dopey frowned.

"Ellie Montgomery from Colorado." He stole the guy's notepad from the desk in front of him and started writing. "Have room service deliver one of those all-in breakfast platters to her room at nine sharp. Include this note, and bill it to my room—the tip, too." He showed his ID and waited for the clerk to look him up.

"Very well, sir." He accepted the note, then read it with a raised brow. "Is there anything else I can help you with?"

The note of sarcasm worried Jax enough that he pulled a twenty out of his pocket and tossed it across the desk. "Don't get forgetful. I might not know where she is, but I can sure as hell find *you*."

Chapter Five

Ellie stretched and eased open her eyes. The brilliant desert morning sun streamed through her window to create a large, luxuriously warm square on the surprisingly plush bedding. It felt good, but nothing like Jax. He'd redefined *good* into some word that hadn't been invented yet. Despite his bad boy exterior, he'd left her floating in a field of warm and fuzzy with the casual way he'd taken her hand. He'd probably done so to lead her through the crowds that clogged the sidewalks, but she didn't care. She wanted to know everything about him, including the way he kissed and where those kisses might lead. *Especially* that, after the way he'd touched her.

Her phone dinged. She unlocked the screen to find the phone where she'd left it...on the picture of her and Jax. His eyes, the shallow blue of packed ice, stunned her. She'd probably see them every time she stood on a mountain in a sea of sky reflecting on fresh powder.

The phone dinged again. Her reverie broken, she swiped

to find a pile of texts from her best friend. She ignored them, opting instead to send the picture of her and Jax. Seconds later, the phone rang. Grinning, she accepted the call.

"That is not the cover model," Taylor said in lieu of a greeting. "But hot damn, he should be."

Ellie fell back into the pillows. "The cover model was… uninteresting."

"Of course he was, and who cares? Who's the guy?"

"He's the cover model's bodyguard. My ticket fell into an auto-flush toilet. Long story short—"

"Um, wait. You can't *long-story-short* the fact that your ticket fell into the toilet."

"It's not interesting, trust me. Anyway, I tried sneaking in the back entrance—"

"You?" Doubt riddled Taylor's voice. "You don't sneak."

Ellie took in the view of the Vegas strip basking in the early morning sun. Her surroundings couldn't be more different from her home among the snow-capped Rockies, but there was something she loved about this city. Even under a sleepy morning sky, the trademark neon faded with the sunrise, Vegas promised excitement. Not that she was one to crave excitement. She sighed. "I'm hopelessly boring, I get it. Anyway, I failed. Security stopped me."

"Security? Like, the cops?"

"No, like the guy in the picture." A carnal thrill shimmied through her.

"Oh, dear God," Taylor said. "Tell me he put you in handcuffs."

"There were no handcuffs. How's Murphy?" The change of subject did nothing to diffuse the heat in Ellie's cheeks, and she suspected Taylor read her like a book. But Ellie could pretty much count on her mutt to give Taylor something to talk about.

"Your dog is a pain in my ass."

"How literally?" Murphy, short for Murphy's Law, had a knack—or more like a life's mission—for getting into trouble at every turn. Ellie first encountered him one snowy day with his tongue stuck to a light pole and the mishaps hadn't stopped since. She'd searched high and low for his owner—only half hoping one would turn up—and had eventually accepted the mutt as her own. Best the vet could guess, he was some kind of lab-Afghan mix. Ellie just figured *gangly mess of trouble* covered it.

Taylor gave a humorless laugh. "All those potted herbs on your window sill over the kitchen sink? Compost."

"How did he get up *there*?"

"I think he was hiding," Taylor said casually. A little *too* casually.

Ellie's eyes narrowed, dimming her view of the city. "In the *sink*?"

"He had his face tucked in the corner. You know how it goes…they can't see you, you can't see them."

"And why exactly was he hiding?" At least Taylor was keeping up with the dishes. Ellie was surprised Murphy fit in the sink at all. It had to have been empty.

Taylor sighed. "You know that really cute delivery guy? He showed up with a box, and I think he might have been flirting with me, but he hit the bricks when that dog started barking. So I might have yelled at the dog. And the dog might have hid."

"In the sink?"

"I think I yelled kind of loudly. Something about how

he'd just killed my chance of seeing the delivery guy's package, if you know what I mean. And when I stopped, I realized the bell was ringing again. Turns out he'd left something in the truck and heard every word I said. So now I have a date."

"Um, you're welcome?" Leave it to Taylor to turn a semipublic spectacle into a date. And the delivery guy certainly was hot, but he was no Jax Mathis. A flush lit Ellie's cheeks. At this rate, she'd set off the sprinkler system.

"Hell, yes, I am," Taylor said. "Although I'm sorry about the herbs. Sort of."

Ellie laughed. "I think it was worth it. Hopefully this guy turns out better than the last one."

"Could he be any worse? And now that we know all about me, back to your guy with the handcuffs. Did you sleep with him?"

The heat of a solar flare touched Ellie's cheeks. Forget the hotel...the entire *city* was in danger of this heat. "There were no handcuffs. And no, I did not sleep with him." In the bright light of day, the idea seemed a little crazy. But last night, in the moment, she wouldn't have said no to anything. And if he were standing in front of her, she had a feeling she still wouldn't.

"Please tell me you are not *that* hopelessly boring."

Ellie shook her head, despite the fact that her friend couldn't see her. "No, he got called into work."

"Are you going to sleep with him tonight?"

"Taylor! I don't...even...*crap*."

"What? What's wrong?"

"I didn't even get his number. He didn't get mine. He didn't ask." All the happy-numbness fled her limbs, leaving dead weight behind. So much for that connection she thought they had.

"Well, you said he got called into work. Maybe he forgot?"

"Maybe." A knock sounded at the door. She looked down and, finding her sleep shorts and tee shirt passable, peered through the peep hole at the same instant the knock repeated.

Startled, she jumped.

"Room service!" a voice called.

"Hang on a sec," she told Taylor before opening the door. As she swung it open, she made a point of saying, "Room service is here. Isn't he cute?" She briefly held up the phone so maybe the guy would think he'd been on camera, even though the camera wasn't on. It was one of the many safety tips she'd learned before her trip. That made her think of Jax, and his random fact memorization problem.

The room service guy blushed.

"I didn't order room service," Ellie said.

"It's a gift. There's a note." He lifted a card from the card and handed it over. "Where shall I set this up?"

"The table is fine."

"What's going on?" Taylor asked. "Who's cute?"

Missing you already, Colorado.

The simple note, followed by a phone number, made her feel ridiculous inside. She absently reached for her purse to tip the guy, but he held up a hand. "It's already taken care of."

"Um, thank you?"

Room service guy let himself out, and she locked the door behind him.

"*El-lie.*" Taylor's voice ratcheted through the phone

Ellie had nearly forgotten she held.

"He sent me breakfast," she said, dazed. "Bacon, sausage, eggs, pancakes *and* waffles, syrup, fresh fruit—"

"How many people does he think he's feeding?"

"Hash browns, biscuits, croissants, jelly, coffee, tea, and juice."

"Well, it's a good thing he didn't forget the juice," Taylor said dryly. "Are you going to tell me about this guy or not? Other than those amazing eyes. Is his body as good as the eyes?"

"The body is definitely as good as the eyes." Ellie picked up a piece of bacon and inhaled, wondering if vacation calories really didn't count. "Like I said, he works security for the cover model. He caught me sneaking into the event last night and told me he couldn't let me in without a ticket, but said if I'd go out with him he'd introduce me to the cover model."

"I gotta tell you, El, he's so hot that's almost not creepy."

"He's absolutely not creepy. And I said if he let me see the cover model *first* then I'd go out with him. And not until."

Taylor's *tsk* whispered through the connection. "Maybe you're not as boring as I thought you were."

Ellie rolled her eyes. "Said with love, of course."

"Of course. And he clearly wants you, so get busy. That's totally permissible there. You know what they say about Vegas."

"Good for Vegas." Ellie sighed and gave in to the urge to eat the bacon. *Divine.* "I like him. I really do, and I'm not someone who can sleep with a guy and forget about him the next day."

"Then don't forget him. Have sex and have amazing

memories. Or have lousy ones, but looking at him, I don't think he's capable of a bad thrust. Point is, no one in your real life will ever know the difference, and you really need to live a little."

He definitely wasn't capable of a bad thrust. The man was too gorgeous for that. "I can't just...proposition him."

"I'm pretty sure he just propositioned *you* by cleaning out the breakfast buffet in your honor. All you need to do is thank him. Profusely and in the nude."

"Taylor!"

"Are you attracted to him?"

"Yes."

"And reasonably sure he's not a serial killer? Or a first-time offender in the making?"

Ellie laughed, mainly to hide her nerves. She was *so* getting talked into this. Perfect little her, who hadn't had any sex at all until she was actual years into what she thought was a committed relationship, was actually considering a one night stand. More than considering, in fact. She was achy and hot over a man. And eating bacon.

The world had upended.

"Reasonably sure," she croaked.

"Then go for it. Have some fabulous sex, then walk away. He could be the biggest jerk in the world—or first in line after your cheating ex, that is—and you'll never know it." Taylor's voice softened. "You've been through a lot. Have something good for once. What have you got to lose?"

"My self-respect?"

Her friend snorted. "I think you gave that up when you tried to sneak in the back door of a black tie event."

"Gee, thanks a lot."

Taylor's *pshaw* tore through the phone. "Get laid, Ellie. And don't come back here until you do."

When Taylor ended the call, the screen switched back to Jax and his bedroom eyes. Ellie had to admit she liked the idea of no-strings sex. She'd had it up to *there* with strings and expectations and emotional attachments.

Maybe Taylor was right.

Ellie swiped the screen. Her thumb hovered over contacts. Adding him seemed a little too permanent, so she opted for her texting app instead. She quickly tapped in the number left on the note, verified she'd gotten it right, and then composed a four-digit message.

Her room number.

Then she hit send.

• • •

Jax spent the remainder of the night sitting in front of Focker's door, mostly counting dots on the carpet. That and checking his phone, despite knowing Ellie wouldn't get his message until morning. By then, Jax would probably be unconscious. Focker had an event at eight, which meant Jax was taking a nap. Period. It also meant if Ellie messaged him, he wouldn't see it until later. The urge to take a cold shower — or ten of them — and wait her out was strong, but if he was fortunate enough to see her later, he wanted to be alert enough to remember it.

As soon as Focker cut him loose, Jax headed to his room. He had a house in the desert, just a few miles off the strip, but staying close to Focker was part of the job. Jax's room was on the same floor, just down the hall. He wondered how close Ellie was. If she thought about him. If she liked him, or if all that talk had been part of the moment…or the game.

Jesus, he was delirious. Either that or back in junior high.

He checked his messages, just in case. Managed to strip down to nothing and toss the duvet off the bed before collapsing.

And he totally forgot to set the alarm on his phone.

He figured that out when he cracked open his eyes to find rays of midafternoon sun piercing the windows. At least he remembered to plug the stupid thing in. After years of being on call for various clients, that particular habit died hard.

He grabbed the device from the bedside table. One message. A phone number he didn't recognize. Followed by an equally unfamiliar four-digit number.

It's her room number, you idiot. Had to be. He grinned and tapped back a reply.

See you there in thirty?

Her reply was immediate. *I'll be here.*

Here, not there. Which meant what? That she'd skipped out on the convention to wait in her room for him? The thought made him stupid-happy. He updated her contact in his phone—*Colorado*—and hit the shower.

Twenty-eight minutes later, he stood outside her room. Nervous. He knocked, and the door opened almost immediately.

He took her in. She stole his breath. Her tan suede boots had some kind of fur trim in the same off-white shade as her sweater. Her pants clung to every curve, and despite that, she managed to look as pure as the driven snow. And this time that prevailing urge to corrupt the hell out of her won.

"I forgot something last night," he said as he stepped into her room. He didn't give her a chance to ask what, just leaned down and brushed his lips against hers, as gently as he could despite the need that tore through him. He resisted the urge to put his hands on her. The brief foray of intimacy they'd shared the night before notwithstanding, he realized she might have second thoughts and didn't want to make her feel trapped. Didn't want to scare her in any way. Just… wanted.

She rested her palms flat on his chest, and for a minute he worried she'd shove him through the open door. He might have deserved as much, but before he could backpedal into an apology, she'd clutched fistfuls of his shirt and hauled him in. She'd surprised him, but by the time her mouth landed on his, he was on board. The tentative exploration of her tongue set him on fire. He roared inside. Devoured her. Tasted heaven.

He slanted his head. Drew her closer. Felt the crush of her breasts against his chest. Resisted the urge to touch them. To grab her ass. To haul her into bed.

So much for good behavior.

He liked her. He definitely wanted her, but he also wanted the chance to get to know her, and that wasn't likely to happen if he threw her down on her bed right then. He didn't want her merely willing to share her body. He wanted her feverish and wet and *begging* for it.

He tried to break free of the kiss and failed. Little parting nibbles turned into more, and she'd only halfway released his shirt. Only then to wind her fingers through his hair, to drag him in and make his dick harder than it had ever been.

"You're not as innocent as you look," he managed to mutter.

"Actually I am," she said, her tone laced with something suspiciously close to regret. "Dreadfully so."

He remembered her words from the night before. "You still looking to misbehave?"

She grinned. "When in Rome."

"Wrong casino, but I can get a room over there if you'd like."

She laughed, and against his better judgment he kissed her again. Breaking free nearly broke *him*.

"I had other plans," he managed. But her room smelled of a fresh shower and the light scent of her skin had him turned inside out. "You can't be all that innocent to make me forget so quickly."

She rolled her eyes. Smiled so damn pretty he hurt inside. "You'd be surprised," she said.

"Actually, I already am," he admitted. "But I'll make you a deal."

A grin softened the lips he'd made swollen with his kisses. "What's that?"

"Spend the rest of the day with me," he said. The need for her to say yes astounded him. Not just because he wanted her, but because he wanted to be with her. His sister's face flashed before him. Trusting. Defiant. *Warning*.

What was he *doing*?

"Didn't we already have that deal?" Ellie asked.

His sister's face faded, but not the guilt. "Yes. No. Dammit."

If she tried to hide her smile, she did a sorry job of it. Thank God she didn't see him for what he was. What he'd been for too damn long to ever change.

He'd failed his sister. He had no right to be happy while she lay in a box in the ground, but he shoved away those thoughts. He'd been given Ellie. A day, maybe two. He could borrow that much happiness, couldn't he? He didn't have to deserve it.

He already had it.

He snagged her hand. Pulled her in. Kissed her. Felt it to his toes, and should have known right then and there he was in over his head, but probably didn't care. It had been too long since someone had walked into his life — all smiles and sunshine — and made him want to bask in anything but guilt.

Only... He broke free, immediately feeling the loss. He took a few steps back before he lost it. "We absolutely do not have that deal."

She looked at him. Confused. Maybe a little hurt.

Asshole. "What I mean by that is I don't want you with me because you feel like you have to be."

His response appeared to only amplify her bewilderment. "Why would I think that?"

"You may have mentioned blackmail as a factor."

Caution broke into a grin. "And then I mentioned Rome."

Her breasts drew his eyes. Why the fuck wasn't she wearing a bra? That sweater of hers was tight knit, loose, but thin. He'd need a straitjacket if those nipples didn't retract. "Rome is most certainly not going to happen because of blackmail."

Humor glinting in her eyes, she asked, "What if I just kind of tolerate you because I want to, and it has absolutely nothing to do with Rome?"

He leaned back against the wall and kicked one foot

over the other. "Just kind of tolerate me, huh?"

She blushed, but she didn't look down. Not this time.

He made her nervous. He liked that. Really liked it. Wished she'd do to him what she was doing to her bottom lip, but if she closed her eyes it would kill him. He needed her looking at him like that.

"I might be willing," she said, edging closer. Or maybe edging for the door. Her nipples were about to poke holes through her sweater. He thought about offering to warm them up for her, but that was for later.

If this was to be the best damned day of his life, that was.

"Good." He reached out and stuck his finger under the hem of her sweater, tugging gently until she obliged his unspoken request. Until mere inches separated them. With him leaning on the wall, his feet stretched between hers, the difference in their heights evened out. He had an unobstructed view of her eyes. Light brown and flecked with color, they reminded him of the desert.

But the desert had never been as beautiful as that.

He cupped the back of her head. Curled his fingers through the long, loose waves that matched her eyes and drew her mouth to his.

She didn't resist. The relief that sweltered through him was short-lived, quickly flamed out by an all-consuming need to taste the rest of her. But he held back. Didn't want to scare her, to see distrust in her eyes.

He slanted his head. Her eyes fluttered closed, and he mourned that until she met him in the kiss. Soft and sweet, nothing had ever sounded better than the tiny sounds of contentment she whispered as he made her his, deepening the contact, savoring the gift. By the time they took a breath she was, for all practical purposes, in his lap, her legs straddling his, his hand still caught up in her sweater. He unwound from the loose hold and reached beneath the fabric. Traced his fingertips against her stomach—not too high, not too low—and enjoyed the quick breath she drew. He kept her gaze. Loved that she didn't seem anxious to look away.

He slipped his hand to her back, his arm still under her shirt, both of them under the same spell. She took the cue and fell into him, soft as fresh-fallen snow. Warm as fuck. She was one pair of jeans and one pair of whatever she was wearing away from riding him, and his balls would probably never forgive him for not mounting up. But for the first time in his life, something more tugged at him. He wanted to know her. Wanted to bask in all that sunshine, to enjoy the innocence before he took that, along with her body.

A lock of hair had fallen in her face. No doubt his fault after dragging his fingers through the strands, so he pushed it back. Almost kissed her again. "I tell you what, Colorado. Let's spend the day together because we want to. I'll try not to want you so hard that I forget to see the desert through your eyes, every damned moment of it, and if you're not sick of me when it's over, I'll take you back to my room or you can take me back to yours."

One of her eyebrows lifted. That strand of hair bounded loose and caressed her cheek, making him want to do it all over again. "And then what?" she asked.

He grinned. "Then you'll find out firsthand what happens in Vegas."

Chapter Six

Ellie almost shook with nerves. She wasn't sure if she'd been rejected or propositioned, but it didn't matter. The day wasn't over, and in fact, Jax had just asked her to spend it with him.

In. The. Desert.

"If you'd rather stay on the strip, I understand. I know you came here for…the convention." His voice, so husky even with such ordinary words leaving his lips, mired her further under his spell.

She shook her head. The haze was still there. Better yet, he was there, hot as sin, sweet as honey. Someone with his rough edges shouldn't be so playful, so ready to smile. "The city will be there tonight," she said. "It's not quite as interesting without the neon." A conclusion that had found her as she stood in her hotel room, staring at the streets below. Waiting for him to reply to her text.

And what convention? She could *not* care less. Not as long as Wolverine remained an option.

"But you don't know me," he said, "and going off grid isn't in the safety handbook."

She looked up, surprised.

He laughed. "I figured if you weren't into walking the strip alone, an excursion to the desert might wave a red flag or two. I probably shouldn't have asked, but what you said about the mountains…that's how I feel out there. I want to share it with you."

She averted her eyes for the briefest moment before zeroing in on him. "Okay."

"Okay?"

"Yes, but I'm telling a friend where I'm going. And with whom."

"I wouldn't expect anything less." He pulled his security ID from his pocket and handed it to her. "Take a picture and send it to your friend."

Ellie accepted the tag and grinned. Or maybe combusted. Even staring straight-faced at the camera, he was smoking hot. The eyes…they were incredible. Taylor would lose her mind.

Ellie probably already had.

"You know," he said, "if you looked at me like that—actual me, not just a picture of me—I'd be a goner."

"I was just thinking the same thing," she said. "But don't think I haven't been."

His brow lifted. A grin touched his lips.

Her stomach dipped, roller coaster style. She shook it off, or at least pretended she could, and snapped a picture of the ID. As she handed him back the card, she asked, "Where are we headed?"

"Valley of Fire," he said. "It's just up I-15 north, less than an hour out of the city. Exit seventy-five."

She tapped out her message and hit send. "If I end up on Dateline, I'm going to haunt you."

"Got a feeling you're going to haunt me anyway, Colorado."

"That's not comforting," she said. But it was. God, it was.

They left her room. She pulled shut the door, then he took her hand. Why did that simple gesture have to feel so good? Why did a guy she was destined to know for three days, tops, have to be so thoughtful?

And she…hadn't been at all thoughtful.

"Oh, no," she said. "I totally forgot to thank you for breakfast."

"I think you already did," he said as they stepped onto the elevator. "Besides, it was more of an apology on my part."

"I didn't eat it all," she said.

He pressed the button for the lobby. "I don't know where you'd have put it. I just wasn't sure what you liked."

"Bacon." She sighed. Or rather swooned. "I never eat bacon."

A corner of his mouth quirked. "Yet you ate the bacon?"

"You ever have bacon with syrup?" she asked.

"If you'd be willing to feed it to me," he said, "and then lay there very still while I lick the syrup off your fingers, I might be willing to give it a try."

And just like that, he'd turned bacon into a sexual experience—one that may or may not ever leave the recesses of her mind, but that she'd relive with every strip of bacon she ever consumed.

The elevator doors slid open to mayhem. At least that's what she thought of the crowds, noise, and lights that comprised the hotel's ground floor casino. Maybe it was the romance convention. Or maybe it was just Vegas. She missed the solitude of the mountains, but now when she pictured being alone there, the image was inexplicably entwined with one of Jax. She suddenly understood why he wanted to show her the desert, because she wanted nothing more than to see the mountains in his eyes.

He led her easily through the melee, so unfazed by it that she had no choice but to believe it was yet another shot of normalcy that, anywhere else, would be anything but.

"How are we getting to the desert?"

"You're already there. But to answer your question, I have a big, black, environmentally disastrous SUV." On cue, they reached the valet. Jax handed over his ticket, and moments later they were met at the door by a jacked up tank. Not *really* a tank, but she doubted anything got in its way.

He waved off the valet with cash and helped her up himself. "Kind of ironic to take one of those out to enjoy nature, isn't it?"

"On one hand, yes."

She ran her fingertips over the soft leather seats and inhaled deeply. "What's the other hand?"

He eased shut her door and didn't answer until he had jumped into the driver's seat. With a firm pat to the dash, he said, "The desert is wide open. You can go pretty much anywhere, and it's better to do it in four wheel drive."

She gawked, and not just because the man was unfairly sexy. He exuded power, navigating with ease onto the busy street. She could probably stare at him all day. In fact, she'd love to get stuck with him, but in the desert? "Mud can't possibly be an issue."

"Nah, but rocks can be." He glanced at the rearview while she admired his profile. "When it does rain," he said, "flash flooding is a thing. Which means swales become one, only they're more like concrete drainage ditches by the time the sun bakes them. You hit one good enough, you'll leave your axle behind in it."

Oh. "So is that what you do? Guard bodies by night and wander the desert by day?"

He shot her a sideways grin. "I guess. Never thought of it that way, but close enough."

She leaned back into the leather and watched the city ease past, surprised to find that a sense of normalcy prevailed away from the strip. Vegas was very much an oasis in the desert—the view from an airplane left no doubt as to the emptiness of the surrounding landscape—but as they left the city, the rearview added a new dimension to the storied location. As wide as the interstate sprawled and as tall as the hotel casinos pierced the air above, the vast desert so quickly consumed the skyline that she wondered if she hadn't imagined the whole place.

But she hadn't imagined Jax. Couldn't have conjured him if she'd tried. It was hard to believe that a mere twenty-four hours before she'd been in the air, high above that very road. Anticipating all the wrong things. If someone had told her that a day later she'd be riding shotgun with a tattooed hottie doing eighty through the desert, she'd have laughed. Or fled.

She certainly would never imagined she'd feel so free.

She caught her reflection in the side mirror and barely recognized herself. Smiling. Sun kissed. Hair all over the place, probably from the breeze that struck while she was hopping up into the truck. Laughing, she pulled it back, then felt the heat of his gaze.

"You're so damn pretty," he said. He paused, looking her way. Hesitant, like he wanted to say something else, but in the end he turned back toward the road.

But she didn't. She watched him, knowing he could feel her eyes on him, but did it anyway. She itched to touch the stubble that darkened his jaw. Already knew what it felt like against her skin. She couldn't forget the softness of his lips or the tenderness with which he explored her mouth. Something deeper had simmered, flaring in his eyes, but he remained so gentle. If it was a strategy, she had to give him credit. Already he had her longing for the crush, for the explosion of demand and utter possession of her body he promised. The tease wasn't enough. Every good girl thing she thought she'd known about herself had been obliterated by this man, and the desire to get closer to him had her vibrating on a frequency that had nothing to do with the hum of the tires on the pavement.

The miles flew, the distant shift of the mountains against the horizon the only real indication of the passing distance. She hadn't realized a world this vast existed outside of her own, that a relatively bare terrain could seem so wild. Or that she could harbor a need so fierce. She ached for him, the desire to be touched coiled so tight she couldn't imagine the force of the explosion.

In no time, they were off the interstate and entering the park. He greeted the guy at the entrance station by name, then rolled through.

"You didn't have to pay?"

"Annual pass. I was here two days ago showing it to the

same man. They know me."

She didn't respond. She was too blown away by the scenery to form words. Red rock and desert scrub stretched as far as the eye could see. And not just any rock, but endless thin layers of sediment that swirled and looped, somehow at once meticulous and wild.

"Wow." She had never imagined nature could be more stunning than the jagged peaks of the Rockies, but then again, she could never have fathomed anything like this.

"Beautiful, isn't it?" he asked softly.

"I almost feel like an intruder."

"You up for a walk? The park is open until sunset."

Sunset. Here. With him. She shivered, though it had nothing to do with the temperature. She'd forgotten her jacket, but the air was still warm. She wished she at least had a bra, but she'd hand-washed her one only to find her luggage suspiciously devoid of another. Not such a big deal for hanging out at her hotel or for the duo of dresses she'd brought for the two formal events she planned to attend, but another issue entirely when she realized she'd be out. With him. She was far from cold—probably too long adapted to what she'd left behind eight thousand feet up in the snowy Rockies—but she knew temperatures fell quickly in the desert. January could be frigid after sunset.

She glanced at Jax and decided there's be no absence of heat in the desert that night.

"I'd love to walk with you," she said.

He steered into the next parking area. His was the only vehicle there. The world was theirs alone, and something about that felt so incredibly right.

She jumped down before he could help her, and with

the chirp of his door lock, they left civilization behind. In some ways, she felt like they'd left earth entirely. The rocks in the park took every alien shape imaginable, from the delicately streaked dunes to arches and columns and beehive formations. The path they walked meandered between rocks, around bends, each turn more breathtaking than the one before it.

"Wait until the sun starts to set," he said. "You'll see how the park gets its name."

"You mean I don't already?"

"Not even close."

They walked a bit longer, eventually stopping at an outcropping with a view of the sun. Already, it colored the sky.

He gestured toward the view, but he needn't. She was already transfixed.

"What you said last night about the mountains made me think of how I feel here," he said. A breeze lifted a strand of her hair. He brushed back the errant piece. Smiled. "Just like you said, then and now. You can't see it and not let it be a part of you."

She swallowed the lump that threatened her throat. She hadn't imagined anyone else could understand what she felt, and she wouldn't have thought it possible that the person who did could have been found in a place that was the exact opposite of hers—a place that could never be her home. They couldn't have been more different, she and Jax, but the connection she felt to him suggested otherwise.

So did the look in his eyes. They captured her, held her for a long moment before he spoke. "What are you running from out there, gorgeous?"

"Not running. Just looking." That old familiar ache returned, and she wondered, not for the first time, why she bothered with the search. Especially now. She'd always been so careful. Had waited to give herself to the man she was going to marry. In retrospect, she could see the relationship wouldn't have worked, and not just because of the horrible way it ended. Maybe she tried too hard to make it something it wasn't. In the end it hadn't mattered, but the failure had left her confused. She thrived on caution. Planning. Every piece had been carefully arranged, only to have all those years of meticulous construction end in a broken heap. It probably wasn't the best way to shape a partnership, but on paper it should have worked. If she couldn't trust a man after three years, how long was she supposed to wait for things to fall apart before she believed they wouldn't?

She looked to Jax. He studied her with such intent, as if her response meant something. How was it possible his eyes seemed to hold so much promise? And what did it matter if they did? Anything they held wasn't for her.

Couldn't be.

She thought about his question. Telling him the truth back to the beginning—that her parents had checked out a long time ago, leaving a little girl to be raised by a string of nannies—had lonely and desperate written all over it. She hadn't any siblings. For as long as she could remember, it had just been her. That a family had been all she wanted, and she'd wasted too many years wanting it with the wrong person. Now her relationship was over, her parents were off playing tourists in Outer Mongolia or somewhere equally absurd, and she'd been left utterly alone.

Inexplicably, she didn't feel that way now. But she

wouldn't admit that, either.

"Have you found it yet?" he asked. "That thing you're looking for?"

She whittled back the hurt and confusion. The pain of so many lost years. It wasn't anything on which she wanted to focus. Not with him filling the void in a way she hadn't thought anyone could—especially not a man who had never been part of her plan. "Sometimes I think it's less about what I've lost and more about what I'm finding along the way."

He looked away. His throat bobbed, and she knew he got it.

"What about you?" she asked.

"I don't know. Sometimes I just get so damn tired of looking."

She reached for his hand, and his fingers immediately curled through hers. "Maybe sometimes you should stop looking," she said. "Maybe, for a little while, just *be*."

He stroked her hand with his thumb. "That's how it feels. Right now, with you."

They stood there for a long while after that, watching the sun crowd the western sky. Every shifting ray of light seemed to bring out a new nuance. Another burst of color.

"Thank you," he said.

"For what?"

"Risking life and limb and Dateline infamy to share this with me."

She laughed.

He didn't.

Instead he leaned down, sparking a firestorm in her that put the scenery to shame. But the anticipation had nothing on the moment he touched his lips to hers, so gently she wasn't sure she felt it. Only that she wanted more.

Visceral anticipation blasted into need and obliterated restraint. She fisted his shirt for the second time that day and dragged him closer. He responded instantly, and the desire he sparked inside her exploded. He devoured her. Flames raged, making her wonder how he could possibly possess her so thoroughly after such a short time. But she'd worry about that later. Right now she had him, his warm, soft mouth owning hers. He held her like he revered her. Treasured her, like she might shatter at any moment. She probably would.

In his arms, the outcome could be nothing less.

When they broke free, they were both breathless. Both hesitant for the distance. She could see conflict stirring up clouds in those crystal blue eyes. Feel the lingering need in the kisses he pressed to the side of her mouth. Knew his desire to stay close by the way his fingers tangled with her hair.

"I don't get you, Colorado." He cupped her head, stroked her cheeks with his thumbs. Claimed her mouth, tugging at her lip with his own. "I don't get you, but I want to. I want you more than anything I've wanted in a long time."

She forced a laugh, probably to hide the fact that she was panting after his kiss. Actually *panting*. His intensity overwhelmed her. Hers terrified her. "I bet you say that to all the girls."

"At the risk of sounding like I'm feeding you a line, only you. And that scares the hell out of me."

Him, afraid? It didn't seem possible. "I can't imagine you being afraid of anything. I mean, you jump in front of bullets for a living." The thought bothered her more than she'd like to admit. It had to be so hard to care about someone whose life was on the line every day.

"For the record," he said softly, "that hasn't actually happened. It's more of a worst case scenario. I'm trained for it, but for the most part these celebrities come to town with an entourage of their own. People they trust. I'm back up, primarily to keep the fans away."

"Like me."

He broke into a grin. "Yeah, like you."

"But you'd still risk your life."

He shrugged and released the tangle of her hair. When he spoke, he addressed the sunset instead of looking at her. "It's the job. Plenty of people risk more every day of their lives. I work a couple days a week and get to hang out in one of the most kick-ass cities in the world the rest. Pretty hard to feel sorry for myself."

She couldn't argue with him, but the undercurrent of his words tore at her. There was something more there. Something that reminded her she didn't know this man.

But she wanted to.

"How did you end up there?"

"In Vegas?" When she nodded, he continued. "When I was a teenager, my parents and I had a...falling out. They decided they were done with me, so I moved in with a friend of mine and his family."

Her attention jerked to his face. She half expected he was joking, the coincidence of abandonment too much, but the pain on his face was real. "Was that when your sister...?"

"Yeah, that was it. My friend's family was nice. Warm people. Good people. But I never got past feeling like I'd intruded, and my buddy was like most kids in that he couldn't wait to get out of there. We had our own reasons, but we were both ready to run. When we graduated we went straight to Las Vegas. Thought we'd have the party of our lives, but we got shut down." He shook his head, a sardonic grin tracing his lips. "Turns out you have to be twenty-one to have any kind of fun there, at least on the strip."

"I suppose getting someone to buy you a twelve pack at a gas station isn't exactly Vegas."

"Not even close," he said with a laugh. "But I fell for the city anyway. Never left. I had enough in savings to get an apartment. Found a job, eventually bought a house."

"How'd you get into guarding bodies?"

"Right place, right time. Didn't take me long to figure out I didn't like being drunk or throwing money into the abyss on gaming, but I love the atmosphere. It's just this batshit crazy place. No one cares who you are or where you're from. You arrive, you're in."

"The party of a lifetime," she murmured.

He nodded. "Every day of the week. Anyway, one of the hotel security guys didn't show up for work one night and they had a big profile client coming in. They knew me. I was there. I agreed to stand in, and they kept me on."

"Just like that?"

"Don't be impressed. It's one step to the left of being rent-a-cop. I don't even carry, although I can lay a guy out with my bare hands in two seconds flat if he wants it bad enough. How'd you get to be a ski instructor?"

She blinked, still stuck on his oh-so-casual *incapacitate a man with my bare hands* statement. He fascinated her. She felt like she was on some kind of out of control roller coaster, every little thing she learned about him an increase in speed in the face of another breakneck turn. The crash at the end was inevitable, but completely worth the ride.

It had to be.

He was watching her, an expectant look on his face.

He'd asked her a question. *Yeah, that.* Memory lane wasn't her favorite place, but somehow he made it easier to go there again.

"I grew up in Colorado," she said. "I've always loved the mountains, mostly from a distance at first. I'd watch for hours through my bedroom window just to see the changing light paint the snow." She laughed quietly. A little bitter, even to her own ears. "It was so much better than TV. My friends thought I was nuts. Anyway, there was this one peak in particular that always fascinated me. I don't know if it was the shape of the rock or the way the snow or the light touched it, but I was obsessed. I'd stare at it and think one day I'd get the summit, and then I'd be free of everything that bogged me down. Kind of silly, I guess."

"But you made it, didn't you?" His voice was full of reverence. Respect.

"I did. Felt like the top of the world, even though it wasn't even the highest peak around."

"Was it what you expected?"

"Yeah, as much as anyone can expect that kind of thing. Problem was, eventually I had to come down. I just never got tired of the summit. Never stopped wanting to recapture that feeling." She gazed off at the horizon, seeing his mountains. She wondered if he ever felt the same way. "I never set out to be a ski instructor. It was more of an excuse to be out there, to be a part of that world."

"Does that feeling ever go away?" he asked quietly.

She looked away from the horizon and found his eyes far more stunning that the painted sky. "I guess if I ever really found what I was looking for, it might."

"You think you ever will?"

"Two days ago, I would have said no."

"What about now?" His words were so serious, they nearly frightened her. Or maybe it was the answer.

"I don't know about that feeling," she said. "Only that right now I'm content to stop looking for what I don't have and enjoy what I do. Right now I'm quite possibly the luckiest person I know."

His expression read *not a chance*. Gave her chills. But he didn't say it. Instead, he said, "I couldn't tell you how many times I've been out here and have stood in this very spot to watch the sun set, but I've never seen it more beautiful than the reflection in your eyes."

"Is that another one of your lines?"

"Nah." He stared nonchalantly at the view as he spoke, but then he tugged at her hand, tipping her just enough in his direction that she landed solidly against him. He released her hand, captured her face. "Don't ever stop looking, Colorado. Don't ever settle for anything less."

She opened her mouth to ask what he meant, but she didn't get the chance before his lips touched hers. Claimed them. Fueled something inside her—a fear that they'd get back to Vegas and she'd lose the night, that the spell would be broken. That he'd have to work. Anything, anything but Rome.

He broke free, only to slant his head and go in deeper. It was that whole tongue-mating thing she'd read in romance novels, only it wasn't some cliché. It was real. So real.

She muttered something unintelligible to her own ears and slid her hands under his shirt. His skin was unbelievably hot. When his abs flexed under her fingertips, she had to fight the urge to peel off his shirt, to see what lay beneath. *Perfect*, that little voice whispered. Had to be utter physical perfection. Could be nothing less.

He returned the favor on the shirt, drawing her close, then taking over. His hard, incredible body was a force, his kisses a demand. And she wanted more.

She wanted everything.

The ache between her thighs turned crippling when he backed her against a rock and worked one of his legs between hers, the sweet tease of the pressure not enough. He'd looped one arm around her back to cushion her against the hard surface, but there was no saving her from him.

He broke free, and for a single terrifying moment she feared he'd back off again. But then he dove in, this time with his free hand caressing her intimately through her pants. She arched against the pressure, whimpering, and felt his mouth stretch into a smile. "You like that, Colorado?"

She couldn't have answered if she tried. She was embarrassingly close to having an orgasm, fully clothed, in public. The sun was low, but not yet touching the horizon, and yet she still had the undying urge to have sex, right there on government property. White-hot need grew and splintered, every jagged edge dragging her closer. And there she was, tearing at his clothes, needing him closer, needing to feel his skin, while he toyed with her.

"I would like nothing more than to fuck you," he said. "Right now."

Good to know we're on the same page.

"But I don't have a condom on me, so I'm going to have to improvise."

She nodded, not even caring what he meant. "Just touch me."

"That's exactly what I had in mind."

In public. Reality gave her a mild slap. Was she crazy? "Is anyone coming?"

"Just you, any minute now." He moved his hand under her sweater, and her nipples tightened painfully in anticipation of his touch. But instead, he flattened his hand against her belly and worked his way south until his fingers were buried between her thighs. "Do you have any idea how much I want to be inside you right now?"

Oh, God oh, God oh, God. "Maybe a little," she managed to whimper.

"Do you like having your nipples sucked?" He asked her so casually, like he wasn't curling his fingers inside her, sending showers of sparks to the edges of her peripheral vision to scatter in the desert breeze. "Do you want to feel my mouth on you?"

Yes. Yes, she did. She nodded. Barely. Maybe. That had never been a thing for her before, but she didn't think there was any way he could touch her that she wouldn't love.

"Lift your shirt."

Arms shaking, she obeyed. The cool air on her bare breasts sent yet another jolt of desire through her, and his appreciation as she bared herself to him left her burning.

He dipped his head and closed his mouth on one stiff peak.

Her knees honest-to-goodness gave out on contact, but he had her. Or she had him. She hadn't realized it, but she was riding his hand like a pony, and the scrape of his teeth against her nipple was making her buck.

And then she was gone. Over the edge with embarrassing speed. She couldn't even pretend otherwise because if he hadn't held her, she'd have landed on the ground in a heap. Was that was orgasms were like? All of the sudden she wasn't sure she'd had one before. Certainly not one like that.

He steadied her. Once she conquered the ability to stand upright, he sat against the rock and pulled her close, wrapping his arms around her against the nearing twilight. "You want my jacket?" he asked when she shivered.

"I want you just like this."

"I was thinking less clothes and a softer bed." He murmured the words against her ear, hugging her tighter, enveloping her in his warmth.

"Look at that sky," she said. Brilliant streaks of orange and red painted the horizon. "Neon's got nothing on that."

"None of it has anything on you, but the park's closing. Ready to head back to Vegas?"

The shiver that overtook her had nothing to do with the air temperature. "Warm bed and no clothes?" she asked. "I'm there."

Chapter Seven

A little more than an hour later, they were back at the Masquerade. Jax handed off his keys to a valet, but Ellie wasn't so quick to jump down from his ride. Instead she peered off toward the corner of the hotel where a huge crowd buzzed the sidewalk.

He rounded the SUV and looked up at her. "Have you seen the show?"

"What show?"

"Come on." Her stance on the truck made it too easy for him to pick her up. He had her on his shoulders before she knew what hit her. She shrieked and laughed, only drawing the barest of attention.

That was Vegas for you. Scary sometimes.

But never so much as the woman who straddled the back of his neck and held his hands for balance. Held more that, but he didn't want to go there. Or maybe he wanted to go there a little too badly. Either way, it was a direction best left unexamined.

Not unlike the Masquerade's fountain show. It was quite possibly the most ridiculous thing in Vegas, which was saying something…especially standing outside the gaudiest hotel to ever cast a shadow over the strip. And there he stood, for the second time in as many days doing something better left to the tourists. But there wasn't a red-blooded man alive who'd fault him. As it was, Ellie drew appreciate glances from more than one passerby. Had to be the pants. Her ass was can't miss, now at eye level to pretty much everyone on the street. The thought was almost enough to make him put her down, but it was he who had landed the spot between her thighs. He might be facing the wrong direction, but she'd chosen him and that was enough.

A cheer erupted from the crowd. Clue numero uno that the reflecting pool outside the casino had started its floor show. He'd seen it more times than he could count. He could practically follow along the choreographed routine by the oohs and aahs alone, despite the fact that he couldn't see anything beyond the beehive of the old woman in front of him. She and her hair stood next to a large man wearing an even more enormous Hawaiian shirt that read *Lost my Shirt in Vegas* across the back.

With that gaudy thing, the guy should be so lucky.

So should the shirt.

Water shot high overhead to a round of applause. Leave it to the tourists to cheer a working fountain. *Running water. Working plumbing. Amazing!* And it only got better, if better meant worse. Soon a Cinderella-style carriage rose from the depths of the pool while a bunch of masked dancers or swimmers or whatever they considered themselves did a

Broadway-reject routine. The whole ordeal would flatline on Rotten Tomatoes if they ever stooped low enough to score sidewalk shows, but the tourists loved it.

When the crowd began to disperse a few minutes later, it was with a great deal of regret that he helped Ellie down from his shoulders. He'd already been half damned feverish from wanting her, and enduring so much body contact only to let her get away was brutal. But they had to eat, so he took her inside the hotel, a little too aware of what awaited him upstairs.

The buffet was packed. Not surprising. People tended to work up an appetite watching all that marauding, or at least that was what one was inclined to think with the way the buffets filled up after the shows. They hit it anyway. Ellie's appetite impressed Jax, but then again, she might have been stalling. He hadn't hauled her straight upstairs because he wanted to give her a chance to change her mind—not because he didn't want her, but because he wanted her to be sure. Now he feared she might talk herself out of taking things further, but he didn't want to push her into anything. He much preferred having her beg. Thinking of how she'd moved against him earlier had him dizzy. And he didn't get dizzy. Or, rather, he never had before.

They left Topenga hand in hand. The casino floor was crowded, most of the tables three deep with gamers. Periodic cheers erupted, though they largely blended with the noise. It was every gaudy, ridiculous thing he loved about Vegas but he barely saw it.

He only saw her.

Only *wanted* her.

He tugged at her hand, and she looked up at him, eyes

shining. For him, or for the lights? "Want to go upstairs?" he asked.

Casual, like it didn't matter, even though suddenly it did. When she smiled, his heart rejoiced.

Wrong organ, dumbass.

But he couldn't bring himself to care. Especially when her gaze tracked below his belt, and his dick jerked like it had been touched.

When her eyes met his, there was none of the uncertainty he feared he'd see. Instead, an assurance when she smiled sweetly, defying all that innocence she possessed, and wrecked him when she said, "I thought you'd never ask."

• • •

Ellie felt a little dirty on the walk to the elevator. Not *dirty*-dirty, but hot-dirty, which may or may not have been a thing in anyone else's life, but was definitely a new thing in hers. Jax walked casually, his fingers once again laced with hers, the fact that one finger had been buried inside her a dirty little secret between them. *So. Much. Dirty.*

"Your room or mine?" He asked so easily, like the question had nothing to do with orgasms between virtual strangers.

"Erm, mine." She didn't want to think about how many other women had been in his before her. Only… "I thought you were local. Why do you have a room?"

"It's just for the weekend. Need to stay close to the job."

She bit her lip, knowing she had to ask the inevitable before she got upstairs and he touched any part of her and made her forget. "Do you have protection?"

"Yeah, I snagged some out of the men's room." She looked at him in surprise, and he laughed. "Sorry. I didn't come here expecting…well, consider it a compliment. Did you ever tell your friend you survived your trip to the park?"

"That's still questionable," she said. But she pulled out her phone to text Taylor, only to find a reply to the original message in which she'd sent a picture of Jax's photo ID.

Lucky, read the reply.

She smiled.

"What?"

She held up her phone for his inspection. Watched his curiosity spread into a grin.

Getting there, she replied. *Made it back to the hotel.*

The phone dinged. *You'd better be limping by morning. In the good way.*

He hit the button for the elevator, then the one for her floor. The ride up was either the slowest or fastest ever—she couldn't decide. Every time he touched her she forgot how crazy it was that she was with him, but there was no getting close enough. No amount of staring at book covers had ever, ever made her feel like this. If Focker had tried any harder to take her upstairs, she'd have knocked him upside the head. But as far as she was concerned, Jax couldn't get her up there fast enough. With him she felt worshipped. Needed.

No one had ever needed her before.

Not like that.

Not like anything.

"You okay?"

She glanced up and wondered how ice-blue eyes could be so warm. She wanted to tell him she was about to be okay, but equally thought she might never be again. "Is this crazy?"

"Crazy by Vegas standards? No such thing."

"What about for you?"

He looked at her until the elevator stopped and the doors sprung open, then he shook his head.

"What?"

"Don't know about crazy, Colorado, but it sure feels right."

His words hit her all squirrely, right in the chest. She agreed. Couldn't agree more. And that, not the sex, was the craziest part of it all.

When they arrived at her room, she slid the keycard and unlocked the door. It felt like ages had passed since they last stood there. And very much like she'd been someone else. Leave it to her to choose Sin City as a place of reckoning.

Once they were inside, he closed the door then turned all that blue on her. "How much do you love that sweater?"

"Um, it's okay?"

He laughed. "There's rock dust on it."

She turned in a useless circle, trying to look at her back. "And you let me walk around like that?"

"Yeah, and I loved every minute. Knowing what I did to you out there, fuck."

"I think that was more of a finger."

He blinked. A grin sprawled. Without taking his eyes off her, he tossed his jacket on a chair and yanked his shirt over his head.

Oh, sweet Jesus.

The man redefined chiseled. His abs had actual ridges. His arms were ridiculous, and the tribal tattoo covering one shoulder and bicep was sexy as hell. With the room deep in shadow, the only light coming in the form of ambient neon through open drapes, his eyes were ethereal.

"Your turn," he said. His tone sent shivers through her that wracked her soul.

She toyed with the hem of her sweater, intentionally stalling to see what he'd do. "What happened to that part where you rip off my clothes?"

He reached into his pocket and withdrew a handful of condoms, then tossed them on the bed without looking. "I've spent half the day touching you and the other half dreaming about touching you, and don't even get me started about last night. I've wanted you every minute. I'm done waiting. I want to see your body. Now."

She was still stuck on the foil packet stash. Was he planning on using all those things on *her*? She counted four. A fifth had flown farther than the rest. And one had slid off and hit the floor.

Six.

Holy shit.

She toed off her boots, hoping she wasn't as visibly shaken as she felt. If she bobbled, he'd know it. His gaze ate her up, and she had no doubt he'd follow suit with his mouth. And soon. Standing there in bare feet, she started to tug at her pants, then remembered the open window. Her gaze darted that way.

"Leave it," he said, apparently aware of the direction of her attention. "Unless it's going to bother you. The lights are off, so no one can see up here."

She eyed the window. "No one without binoculars."

"People don't carry those anymore. They just use the zoom on their cell phone cameras."

"Funny guy." She took a few deliberate paces from the window, then stepped out of her pants.

He sat on the end of the bed, legs sprawled. Bulge noticeable. His chest was mostly bare, probably too chiseled for more than the few intrepid hairs to grow. It's not like the stuff could sprout through steel, although he did have a nice dusting of happy trail between his belly button and his belt. And his V lines could cut butter. This man should be in his underwear on every billboard in America, but he wasn't.

He was on her bed.

Waiting for her.

"Take it off," he said softly. "Let me see you."

She was so nervous. And turned on beyond belief. He looked at her as if he'd found religion, and that scared the hell out of her. How was she supposed to forget something like that?

Slowly, she peeled off the sweater. She thought she heard an intake of breath from his direction, but by the time she had the fabric over her head, no evidence remained. Now she was down to her thong, and the only reason for that was because Taylor had apparently swapped out Ellie's actual underwear for dental floss when she wasn't looking. *No one wears granny panties in Vegas*. She could still hear the admonishment. Had no idea when her friend had subsequently snuck into her luggage, but at the moment Ellie was eternally grateful. Sort of. Being so close to naked was terrifying, but standing there in granny panties would be mortifying. The difference mattered. Thank goodness the pair she'd worn on the flight in were hanging in the bathroom with her bra. She'd have to sneak in there before he did so she could hide them. Maybe in the garbage.

"Come here."

She did, adding a little bit of sway to her hips.

He watched like he was attempting to memorize every move. "Do you have any idea how beautiful you are?"

She hoped it was a rhetorical question.

"Can I touch you?"

She hoped that wasn't. "Yes."

He didn't. Not at first. Not while her nipples tightened into painful peaks and the scent of her arousal permeated the air. *Not awkward at all.* Finally he reached for her and took her hands, pulling her onto the bed so she sat on her knees, straddling him. Every inch of her body screamed to be touched, but it was her breast, aligned so perfectly with his mouth, that gained his attention. When he sucked in her nipple, all heat and tongue, she grabbed for his head, thinking she was steadying herself. Then she realized she was pulling him in, adding pressure, begging for more. And he gave it. The way he worked his tongue on all that sensitive flesh had her grinding on his jeans. The effort was futile. Mere denim couldn't touch what he'd done to her earlier with his fingers, and now that she was a little more familiar with his mouth, she knew she was screwed. The idea that she could survive on one night with this man was ridiculous.

The idea that she could survive a night without him, more so.

It was a dangerous road. A thrilling one.

One she wanted to ride for all it was worth.

He swapped sides. Somehow. She hadn't let go of his head, and she was still riding him through his clothes. His self-control was ridiculous. She'd have sold her soul in that moment for an orgasm, and he was just toying with her. If only he'd toy with her *there*…

She leaned back, escaping his mouth. He fastened his gaze on her, then wordlessly pulled her into a kiss. Madly, deeply, he explored her mouth, his hands on the small of her back, pressing her body against his. His skin was soft, his muscles hard, the heat unbearable. She had never wanted to come so badly that it hurt not to, but this need crippled her. The ache was almost a pain, the wait nothing short of agony.

"You want me, baby?"

"Yes." The understatement of the millennium. And he asked so innocently she might have laughed if she weren't so riddled with an absolutely nonnegotiable need to hit the big O. She probably would have sounded maniacal, à la *The Shining.* Yeah, that was sexy.

But dear God, Jax was. He grinned and stood, taking her with him. Then he turned, switching positions with her so it was she over the bed, and eased her onto the mattress. When he backed away, she almost cried out for him. Then she noticed his attempt to get out of his jeans and thought better of it. He actually winced as he worked the zipper, and she realized she wasn't the only one wanting. Or naked underneath. "You go commando?"

"Not the best idea today," he said, "because I don't think those teeth marks are coming out, but yeah." *Teeth marks?* He won the battle with the zipper—*oh,* those *teeth*—and shucked his shoes and pants.

And she could only stare, mouth open, at the whole nine yards.

Nine yards. *Holy…*

The thing was a beast. *Of course it was.* No way a man as hot as Jax would pack light. Nature couldn't be that cruel.

Or maybe it was precisely that cruel. Stupendously so.

"I'm not sure…"

He leaned past her and grabbed a condom, then managed to turn rolling it on into a seduction. Just the thought of that thing in her made her ache. Both ways.

When he stood, he pulled her to her feet. "C'mere."

He looped his thumbs at her hips down her thong, then eased the strings down, first one side, then the other. At some point he must have let it fall, but his hands held their course. His palms flattened against her butt. She'd have been a little paranoid if his expression hadn't taken on that of someone who had just tasted something delicious, which at least in her mind meant he liked what he saw. He must have liked it a lot, because all that yummy contentment melted into something dark and wild. Jax being cute and sexy was one thing, but feral Jax was a force. Feral Jax could move mountains with his eyes alone.

The thong out of his way, he sat on the bed and once again tugged her to his lap. He gestured for clearance, so she got to her knees. When he grabbed his erection and positioned it under her, she caught on. He wanted her on top.

She had never, ever been on top before. Had no idea what to do. But she was unbelievably wet at the prospect, and he was already there, probing her entrance and damned if she didn't want to figure it all out.

He watched her intently, and the rest of her world faded away. She trusted him. Coveted him. Would probably build a shrine to him when it was over. No one had ever looked at her in such a way. No one had ever made her feel treasured, like the world wouldn't turn another inch without her in it. The thought of leaving that behind made her want to crumble, but fortunately she had a freaking redwood there to hold her up. All she had to do was climb on.

Yep. That was it. *Just. Climb. On.*

Anticipation assaulted her until she no longer had a choice. She eased her weight onto him and couldn't stop the gasp of pure pleasure that erupted as he filled her. Just a couple inches down, then back up. Further the next time. Her body screamed at the pace, wanting more. Her resolution that she could never, ever take him disintegrated. She wanted him. All of him.

His hands were on her hips, not pushing, but guiding her. He didn't give her a chance to sit there and figure out what to do next. He was already there, rocking her with a gentleness that belied the punishing, possessive desire that tore through her. The realization that she'd taken his entire length stunned her, but she didn't have time to wallow in it. The sensations were too pure. Too much. The pressure on her clit was exquisite. Relentless. The pace increased, and she wasn't sure who to blame. Just knew that she shattered before she'd even broken a sweat. She was only vaguely aware of him flipping her over and rolling into her, muttering profanity as his hips rocked against hers, then jerked. She felt that to her core, his body driven so deeply into hers that he'd become a part of her.

Her very favorite part.

"I'll be able to move again in a minute," he muttered through jagged breaths. "Which is about one minute longer than that took."

She blinked away the sparks that dotted her vision. The ceiling spun. It looked like one of those time lapsed astronomy photos, all swirls and light. Either she couldn't handle her orgasms, or she couldn't handle Jax Mathis.

But she'd learn.

"If I counted right," she said, "you still have five chances to redeem yourself."

"I'm sure there are more where those came from," he said. The mattress muffled his voice.

She laughed. Tangled her fingers in his hair. Stretched beneath him, luxuriating under his weight. He was solid. Strong. *Hers*. Maybe not that last part, but she wanted it. Wanted it so badly.

She absolutely sucked at one-night stands.

Too quickly, he eased his weight from her, crawling backward. Away. She watched him for only a second, then let her head fall back to the pillow. She closed her eyes and tried to memorize every sensation, but already her thoughts offered no relief. She'd just come harder than she ever had in her life, and already she wanted more.

She vaguely registered that he headed for the bathroom and figured he had to dispose of the condom. *One down, five to go.* A moment later he was back, his hands pushing aside her knees. His mouth on her. She swallowed a scream—the good kind—as he tasted her. Thoroughly. Each brush with her sensitized clit was more crippling than the last. Two laps of his tongue later, she was clutching the bedding, torn between spreading her legs further and clamping her thighs against his head. Either option sounded fantastic, but she didn't have the wherewithal to make the choice. She felt like she'd grabbed an electric fence. With her teeth. "This is almost cruel," she managed.

"Faster than a shower," he said, grinning, and plowing deeper. Not as deep as he'd been moments earlier with the mighty redwood, but with more dexterity. Soft, then rough, working her with both sides of his tongue until she'd all but ripped the sheets from the bed. Orgasm claimed her, quietly, leaving her whimpering. Less needy, more exhausted.

Totally, absolutely wrecked.

Chapter Eight

Ellie dozed.

Jax watched her, unsure if he'd ever put a woman to sleep before. Even more unsure how to take it. He knew he'd lost all sense of rational existence when she'd taken his cock. Knew she'd wanted him because she was slick as fuck. Knew she'd come because every spasm had jacked him. It had been scary good—so good he half worried the force of how good it was had torn through the condom. Fortunately, it had remained intact.

Him, not so much.

She was perfect. Something that didn't exist in his life. Couldn't. But there was no other word for her. Not just the sex, although there were no words for that, either. There was just something about her. Something that scared him.

He tried to pick it apart. She wasn't the only woman who smiled at him. Wasn't the only one with an infectious laugh. Not the only one wary of Vegas and clueless on slots. She was just…Ellie.

The door beckoned him. *Get out, buddy*. He should. He had a rule against overnights. But he also had her, if only for one more day, and he wasn't quite ready to let go of that broken piece of him that felt dangerously close to salvation.

He stared beyond the glass to the city below, and for the first time felt like a stranger in it. Vegas was so all-fucked crazy that anyone could belong, but he didn't feel that way then. His gaze skated to Ellie, to the long, sleek lines of her body and the sweet innocence of her face. She had a phenomenal ass. Sensual lips. Smart, funny, total package.

Run.

Not likely. Not yet. He'd missed that boat when he arranged to meet her after Focker's shindig.

Rather than leave, he helped himself to her shower. He turned on the spray and stood there, wondering how it was possible he'd known her for a couple of days. Not even that long. It felt like ages ago that she'd showed up, all wide-eyed and clueless about Focker. Jax had rolled his eyes to high heaven over having to babysit the pampered cover model, but now it felt like the biggest break of his life.

Or was it the worst?

He did a once-over with the soap. His dick begged for more than the flimsy attention, but he ignored it. He'd feel like an ass if she walked in there and caught him, although the idea sparked a new fantasy—one where she'd drop to her knees and look up at him with those big brown eyes as she sucked him dry.

Oh, yeah. He was so far beyond screwed he'd need a road map to find his way back.

He toweled off, then pulled on his jeans and ordered

room service. They'd just eaten not too long ago, but he had bacon on his mind. Bacon and syrup. As soon as he hung up, he went to Ellie and worked the blankets out from under her so he could cover her. He hated to do that, but he'd also hate to bust up the room service guy for seeing her naked, so he kept with the plan.

While he waited he flipped channels, eventually settling on a crime show. It reminded him of her Dateline concerns and the fact that she had trusted him. He was in some kind of bad shape if he couldn't watch a forensic report without thinking about her. Wanting her.

What the hell happened here?

He was saved from having to answer his own question when the food arrived. He tore into the pancakes, leaving a couple of them plus the bacon for her. Syrup for dessert.

"Do I smell bacon?" she asked, her voice sleepy. Sexy.

He didn't look at her. Just broke into a smile that surprised him. "Welcome back."

"Seriously, is there bacon?" She sounded more alert now.

He handed her a piece over his shoulder. "I don't know why you parted ways with bacon, but I think it's time you stage a reunion."

She crawled across the bed, settling next to him on the foot. "Haven't I?"

"What about when you leave here?"

The question took on a meaning he never intended. It hung there heavily, a white elephant in a gaudy hotel in a room that smelled deliciously of swine.

"About the bacon, I mean."

"I think I'll still want it," she said softly.

He wasn't one of those intuitive types, but he was pretty sure she wasn't talking about the bacon. He swallowed whatever that threatened to mean to him. "I'm not finished with you, you know."

"Is that a warning?"

Remembering what she'd said earlier about syrup, he dunked a piece of bacon and handed it to her. "Yep."

He glanced back in time to see a drop of syrup fall, landing just north of her left nipple. She swiped it with her finger, then stuck her finger in her mouth and licked it. When she saw him watching, she blushed, all kinds of pretty.

His cock hardened. No warning, not much chance of hiding it, but thank God for the jeans. He wasn't a connoisseur of dick sizes. Had no idea his was worthy of alarm, but he believed her reaction genuine. The woman was unbelievably tight. Absolutely made for him. Her wariness over the size of his junk wasn't something he wanted.

Neither was one night.

He wanted more. Wanted them all.

Nope, nope, nope.

Couldn't go there. He'd already lost too much, and in doing so he'd proven himself unworthy. Logically he knew better than to think he could have her outside of the bed-room—and the weekend—but he couldn't relegate her to anything less than something meaningful. They may not be going anywhere with this, but she was no one-nighter. Not by a long shot.

His affirmation hadn't fazed her. Not like bacon. She held out her hand, clearly not reaching for him. But he took her anyway, closing his mouth on her fingers and sucking them in until he'd eradicated every last trace of bacon. When he released her, she stared, dazed, as he swirled another piece of bacon in syrup and handed it over.

She took it and without breaking eye contact brushed her nipple, leaving behind a trail of syrup. "Your turn."

Oh, hell no. He used all the restraint in the world to not throw the plate down. Not dive in. And then he figured out how to use all that restraint to his advantage. He wasn't going down in fewer than ten thrusts. Not this time.

She sat on the bed on her knees, gorgeous. Syrup drizzled down her breast. A drop actually beaded on her tight nipple, the little bastard. He bypassed it to take her hand, then he again sucked her finger into his mouth. When the flavor was gone, he worked on her thumb. The drop of syrup on her nipple held on.

"You aren't as innocent as I thought you were," he murmured, tugging her to her feet.

"Trust me, you've done all the corrupting."

"Good." He bent down, cupped her breast, and trailed his tongue over the syrup. He wanted so badly to take the whole thing in his mouth, but the night was going too fast. He wanted to know more than her body. He wanted to know *her*, and that was terrifying.

Too bad it didn't terrify him enough to keep him away from a phallic meltdown, but he'd figure that out. They had all night.

One damn night.

He must have shaken his head. Looked at her in a certain way.

"You don't want to do this?"

"Funny thing," he said. "I can't think of what I've ever wanted more. Scares the hell out of me."

She blinked once. Then about ten more times. Then she scooched off the bed. "I'll be back in a minute," she said.

"Okay." Only it wasn't. He had no clue what he'd said. Or hadn't. He watched her walk, attention pegged on her ass, until she disappeared into the bathroom. Why had she chosen that moment to walk away? Was she feeling what he felt? He ached with the reality of this mess he'd gotten himself into. He was afraid to stay. Just as afraid to go. Did she want him out of her room?

He turned toward the view of the city. Barely recognized it. The landmarks were there, but something inside him had changed. Something inside him that needed her. But he couldn't do that—he'd avoided connections far too long. This one had slipped past him. Thrown him.

He sensed her presence before he heard her. Before she slid her arms around his waist from behind and rested her head against his shoulder. She wore a shirt. The realization hit him hard. Regrets already?

So many questions assaulted him, but one hit harder than the rest. One mattered more. He tried to push away the importance it held, but all he managed was to ask, "You think you'd ever leave Colorado?"

"I never even thought about it before." She left the rest unspoken. *She had now.* "You think you'd ever leave Vegas?"

He stared through the glass, the knowledge strong that he stood inside a building that looked like it had fallen off a trailer at Mardi Gras. On the strip, among palaces and pyramids and scaled down versions of the Statue of Liberty and the Eiffel Tower, the Masquerade didn't stand out. Much. But just a block to one side or the other, the view was almost normal. Casinos were scattered throughout the city, but off strip they tended to wear the neon with a bit more subtlety. Of course, subtle compared to the deep fried vat of crazy that was Las Vegas Boulevard probably wouldn't qualify anywhere else in the world, but here, it was a thing.

"I don't do mountains," he said. He still wouldn't. Not even for her.

He turned to draw her into his arms, to soften his words, and was surprised to discover the shirt she wore was his. Seeing her like that made his heart do funny things in his chest—things he didn't want to examine too closely.

"Funny thing about mountains," she said. She traced the lines of his tattoo as she spoke. He wondered if she looked at it and saw what he did. What he couldn't forget. "Some people just stand at the bottom and talk about how big they are, never once believing they could get to the top. And some people aren't afraid of the climb, but of what they'll see when they get there." She looked from the artwork on his arm to his face. "Some people are just so afraid of falling that they won't even try."

"What about the ones who do fall?" he asked. "Those who hit the ground hard and are just too damned broken to get back up again?"

"Is that what happened to you?"

Him. Gracie. Same damn thing. He hadn't quite realized that before. Sixteen years later, and neither one of them were living. "Not every wound can be healed."

"I saw you out there in the desert," she said. "I saw your face. You found something out there, and it scared you. That's why you come back to this city, isn't it? Because nothing here is real."

Her words cut a little too close for comfort. Stung like

a bitch.

"You're real," he said. It sounded a little more like a protest. An excuse.

She smiled, but it didn't reach her eyes. "No, Jax. I'm not. I'm Colorado."

He closed his eyes. She was right. She couldn't be real—not if he had any chance of standing upright when she left—but at that moment he wished on every star in the sky that she could be. But what did that matter? The stars didn't exist there. Not the real ones, not over the glow of the neon. "Why did you put on the shirt?"

"Because you scared me."

Her response startled him. "In what way?"

"You said *you* were scared. And here I've been thinking I'm just gullible or clingy or whatever makes people boil rabbits after a one-night stand and that it was just me. But then you said it was you, too, and I just don't know what to do with that."

"Who the hell boils rabbits after a one-night stand?" he asked. "Is that actually a thing?"

"It's a thing in a movie," she said. "And I can barely stand to scramble eggs, so you're safe."

Yeah, sure he was. Only apparently neither of them felt that way. "I'm sorry," he said. "I didn't mean to scare you."

"It's not that. Not exactly. It's just…I was engaged once."

Great. Just what he wanted to hear.

She frowned, and he wondered just who she saw in her mind's eye. "He was the first person who ever wanted me," she said.

Jax severely doubted that, but he didn't interrupt.

"I waited forever. Took it slow. I used it as some kind

of test of his love—that if he was willing to wait for me, he must really love me. And he waited. Said he'd wait forever as long as he had me in the end. I fell. So hard. When you spend most of your life feeling like no one needs you, that's pretty much the best thing a person can say. *I need you. You're worth the wait.*"

Well, good for that bastard. Jax hated him already. "So what happened?"

"He only waited with me. Had a girl on the side who kept him entertained because I wouldn't—one he didn't give up when I gave in. Three years into our relationship and a month after I lost my virginity to him, I walked in on them. I was devastated. And the worst part was it wasn't some frantic, torrid thing. He held her in a way he never held me. I actually stood there for a minute before they noticed me. I stood there and thought, why can't I be loved like that?"

"Oh, God, Ellie."

"Yeah, well, I snapped out of it pretty quickly. They're still together, but I don't think they'll be having any children—at least not the old-fashioned way."

He ached for her. Wanted to pulverize the asshole who had hurt her in such a way. But more than anything, he wanted to fill that void.

He wanted to be the one who loved her like that. Could he? He'd learned a long time ago he wasn't someone who could be trusted, but those old lessons had no place here. He wanted to be that man. He wanted that for her.

The need raged quietly, fueling something he didn't know he had to give. And suddenly he didn't care how he'd manage when she left. He stood on the edge of that, on the edge of giving in and giving everything, when she spoke.

"I waited so long. *That* was supposed to be right. This should be what feels wrong, but it doesn't." She ran her fingertips down his chest. Spoke quietly. "One night was never supposed to feel like this."

"Baby, it shouldn't feel like anything less."

He kissed her then, all the fire a barely restrained torrent. He actually shook with the need to consume her, but he held back. Held her. Held on. Nothing in the world had ever felt better than having her body aligned with his, his fingers tangled so gently in her hair, her mouth his own. He could taste her growing urgency, feel her heat. He walked her backward to the bed, stripping her of the shirt as he went. He pushed the bedding out of the way, then lay her down on the cool sheets.

She watched intently as he lost his jeans and tore open a condom. He rolled it on, then crawled on top of her, pulling the blankets over his back and he lowered against her. Into her. She held his gaze as he entered, a little at a time, each push punctuated with a tiny withdrawal until they had joined as completely as two people ever could. The blankets added to the softness and warmth, making their small world their own. There was no Vegas. No mountains to climb. Just one man and one woman, everything on the table, nothing left to give.

She clutched his shoulders as he shook with the restraint required not to drive into her. Held on as he rolled his hips. No grinding, no fucking. Just the sweet bliss of being the one she'd chosen, if only for a night.

If only to forget.

Desire rocketed through him, the intentionally slow pace more brutal than any he'd ever known. He shifted, nudging deeper, feeling her leg slide the length of his. She arched against him, baring her neck, and he claimed the spot with his mouth. Fingernails raked his back, but still he held on. He tried not to think about what she was doing to him. What she allowed him to do to her.

Her body enveloped him, all heat and fire, and he held her with everything he had. Kissed her neck. Nibbled her ear. All the while, driving into her, rocking his hips, pistoning longer, slower, deeper. Breaking a sweat, tasting that she'd done the same.

And kissing her. Dear God, the sweet slide of her tongue with his was enough to leave him undone. He explored every crevice, tasted every part of her, swallowed every whimper. Forced himself to take her deeper, pushing against the bed with one knee, gaining traction. Nudging her across the sheets with his desire to consume her, to so thoroughly become a part of her body that he'd be there forever. He knew the moment she came. Knew she hadn't been thrown off some cliff to flail, to seek purchase from thin air. That wouldn't happen, not this time. He gave her something to hold on to while she trembled. Kissed her. Touched her hair, cupped her face. Held on until his own orgasm took over, stealing his sense of self, leaving him shaking and lost.

Lost, with no real desire to be found.

When he went to the bathroom to clean up, he didn't recognize himself in the mirror. Didn't recognize what raged inside him.

Didn't matter.

Just went back to the bed and held her, knowing it had to be enough.

Knowing damn well it'd never even come close.

Chapter Nine

Gracie pulled at Jax's arm and batted her baby blues. "Please, Jax? Just one more run. Mom and Dad will never know."

He shook his head. "No way. We'll be late, and they'll blame me."

"No one is gonna blame you. Just tell them the line for the ski lift was long. Please?"

Jax blew a frustrated breath that pillowed in a cloud in front of his face. "It's too warm."

"Don't be ridiculous. If it was too warm, they'd close the mountain. Besides, you can still see your breath."

"That doesn't mean it's cold enough." But still, Jax teetered on the verge of giving in. He had a hard time denying his baby sister anything, but if he greenlighted Gracie and his parents found out, they'd never trust him again.

"One run. I'll be fast."

He sighed. "I know you will. Go ahead. I'm right behind you."

She squealed and managed to leap into his arms, nearly toppling them both. By the time she wriggled down, their skis were entangled, and they both ended up in the snow. "You're a twerp," he muttered.

She flashed one of her effervescent smiles, then clamored to her feet and checked the straps. They rode the chair lift to the top of the mountain, Gracie chattering the whole time about skiing a new black diamond trail earlier that day. About wanting to do it again.

"Don't even think about it," he warned. "Stick to something easy. If you break your neck, I'll never hear the end of it."

The lift deposited them at the top of the mountain. She leaned down to check her skis one more time, then dropped her goggles into position. "Think you can keep up?"

Jax checked his equipment. "No problem."

With a mischievous grin, she kicked off for a nearby intermediate trail. He followed behind her, slowly realizing the snow was too wet in the sun. Unease crawled through his chest. "Gracie!"

He looked up in time to see the little imp make a sharp turn onto a black diamond slope. The move required skill — there was no way it was an accident.

"Gracie!"

Either she didn't hear him or she'd ignored him, not that it mattered. You couldn't ski backward up a mountain that steep, so he pushed his misgivings aside and took the turn after her. He wasn't entirely confident he was up for a black diamond run, but there was no way he was leaving his baby sister to fend for herself. The sun beating onto the snow worried him.

"Gracie!"

She slowed, and he relaxed a notch. Then she took a hard turn and headed off the trail.

Off. The. Trail. Against the rules. There was no way their parents wouldn't find out about this.

"Son of a bitch." Jax had no real business on an expert trail, let alone off one. He stood there, trying to catch his breath and wondering what he should do. If he called ski patrol, they'd both be in trouble. But he couldn't just let her go out there alone. Growing frantic, he searched for someone. Anyone. But they were alone on this side of the mountain.

Just him and the lukewarm sun and Gracie's bright red beanie weaving down the mountain...then a rumble. Low at first, then thunderous.

Then she was gone.

"Gracie, no!"

Everything happened in horrible, slow motion. A massive sheet of snow slid, then broke and tumbled, taking Gracie with it.

Jax stood frozen. Searching. The mountain settled into silence.

Ellie was gone.

Ellie.

Jax's eyes flew open. He was drenched in sweat. Shaking. Ellie slept next to him, seemingly unaware that she'd invaded his dreams.

Dreams. More like the worst fucking day of his life. Only now it wasn't just Gracie he'd lost, but Ellie. Even though she was right there, his heart constricted. Ellie loved those damn mountains. She was a *ski instructor*. He'd loved Gracie, and that hadn't been enough to keep her alive. He'd stood there and watched her disappear. It hadn't mattered that he'd hauled ass down the mountain for help, or that she should have known not to go off the trail. She wouldn't have been there at all if not for him. He deserved every ounce of the pain.

He couldn't go through that again. He'd relive it every time Ellie stepped foot on a mountain—Gracie being gone, Ellie being next.

She was so beautiful. So peaceful. He thought of Gracie and her smile, but only saw Ellie.

He couldn't lose her…not like that. Not even after what they'd shared.

Fuck.

He eased from the bed, every muscle tight. Trembling. He once again helped himself to her shower and cranked the water as hot as he could stand it. The stall was devoid of the hotel's mini-bottles, so he settled for Ellie's shampoo, realizing too late that he'd never escape her with her scent enveloping him.

Fuck, fuck, fuck.

He needed to think…about anything other than the way they'd fit together. But that was all he saw. All he felt. He'd never done that before. Never touched a woman like that. Had never been touched. It wasn't sex.

It was possession.

God, how he needed her. And the more he realized it, the more the red flags waved. He couldn't be that man for her. She deserved more. She deserved someone who had something to give, and that wasn't him. Never would be.

He let the water run, hoping it would take the last traces of honey-citrus-whatever with it. Hoping it would take the pain of wanting what he couldn't have.

A happiness he didn't deserve.

He couldn't protect his sister. He couldn't protect Ellie.

He shut off the water and dropped his forehead against the tile wall. Thought of her smile, of how she lit his world. She was sunshine personified. She made the simplest things special. Walking the strip. Slot machines. Syrup.

Already his mind spun with the possibilities of having and holding her. Of being a different person all the time, not just when she was around. But he couldn't risk that. He couldn't risk her happiness.

He couldn't risk falling in love with her.

Realizing he was cold, he yanked down the nearest towel and slung it around his hips. Walking into the suite felt like stepping into a minefield. He didn't want to be an ass and disappear, but he wasn't ready to face her. Not when she'd have that look in her eyes. Not when that look was one he craved.

He managed to get his pants on before she stirred. His shirt before she spoke.

"Are you leaving?"

He hated that she had to wake without him in the bed. He wanted to be there with her, to feel every satiny inch of her skin stretched against his. Before the nightmare, he'd slept so well with her tangled with him, fitting in his arms like she didn't belong anywhere else.

He'd come that close. That damn close to a chance of happiness.

"I need to go," he said. Simply. Truthfully.

She squinted against the light. "Can I see you later?"

"The ball is tonight," he said. "I have to tail Focker."

"Well, then, I guess…thank you?"

He felt like an ass. Tomorrow was Sunday. She was leaving, and he'd just blown her off. "Meet me in the ballroom at five. I'll buy you a drink. Maybe help you snag a dance with your cover model." If Focker even danced.

Her eyes narrowed, then shot daggers.

He turned away, knowing damn well why she was pissed. When he met her, he'd wanted nothing more than to turn her off the guy, but now…he should have left well enough alone. Jax, on the other hand, had gone and made it personal. Ellie had opened her heart to him, and he'd probably never shake the repercussions.

More guilt. Right up his alley.

"That was the deal, right?" His words sounded lame, even to his ears.

"Not good enough," she said. Softly, but with a dangerous edge.

He slid his feet into his shoes and patted his pockets. Felt like he had everything. Knew damn well he didn't.

Knew he didn't have her.

"I'm sorry if that's not good enough, Colorado, but it's all I've got." He eased from the room and tried to forget the expression on her face.

Knew he probably never would.

The door that shut behind him sounded more like a prison cell. Only it wasn't her in the cell…it was him. And for the first time, he had a glimpse of the other side, and he wanted out. He wanted one night to turn into ten. Hell, he wanted them all.

But what they had wasn't real. Nothing in Vegas was real, and Ellie had nailed him on that point. But he'd never wanted more. Not until her. All he knew how to do was walk away from sex, but what they'd shared had gone so far beyond sex. He would have chalked it up to that whole "What happens in Vegas…" nonsense, but they'd both been stone sober. Whatever happened between them *counted*. It meant something. Sex had always been a one-off kind of thing. But with her, he wanted the intimacy they'd somehow captured. Wanted her smile. Her laugh. The feel of her silky limbs stretched along his length. He wanted her friendship. To look forward to seeing her name pop up on his phone.

He wanted it all.

He couldn't say he'd spent his life walking away from emotional entanglements because he'd sure as hell never come close to feeling whatever he felt for her. After one night, it scared the hell out of him, but he wanted it. He fucking *wanted* it.

But worrying about it was moot. No matter how much he wanted otherwise, theirs was a one-night thing. A weekend at best…a weekend with a *ski instructor* of all damned things. He just couldn't go there. He couldn't let himself care about someone who loved what he feared the most.

Didn't matter how he felt. They'd never climb those mountains together.

The sooner he got a grip on that, the better.

• • •

Ellie stared at the door long after it shut behind Jax. Part of her ached for him, for whatever put the sorrow in his eyes, but a bigger part wanted to kick his ass. After what they'd shared, how could he even begin to think she still wanted anything to do with Focker? She didn't care about the cover model or the ball or anything having to do with the convention. She cared about Jax. About stripping the sorrow from his eyes and making him smile again. He needed that. He needed *her*, and dammit, she needed to be there for him.

He knew it, but he'd closed down. Shut her out.

When she was growing up, her family had been distant. Closed off. She'd had every material thing she could have asked for, but she didn't have their love. She hadn't made a difference in their lives. But she could see the difference in Jax. He'd admitted as much, and in her twenty-eight years she'd learned that meant something.

Mattering to someone *meant* something.

But not if he didn't want it.

She showered and dressed and hit the strip. By day, the hotels and casinos that lined the famed parts of Las Vegas Boulevard were almost normal in appearance. A little over the top, for sure, but the Masquerade really stood out with its brightly colored balls and ribbons. The carnival-like display made Circus Circus look subdued in comparison, which was saying something, considering the latter was built in the image of a circus tent.

Everything she saw reminded her of Jax. Couples held hands. Slot machines dinged. Hotel rooms loomed overhead.

What had gone wrong?

She'd seen enough movies to know the morning after tended to do a number on the events of the night before, but there were no expectations between her and Jax. He hadn't made any promises. Hadn't offered her the world.

He'd just given it to her.

She blinked back the sudden heat in her eyes. She had no idea what compelled her to tell him about her miserable experience, but he hadn't run. That would have been too easy. Too merciful. Instead he'd given her soap opera sex. He'd devoured her with a tenderness she couldn't have imagined. Encompassed her, body and soul, with the kind of warmth and passion that only happened in movie scripts. But there'd been nothing scripted about it. Just a sweet, heartfelt posses-sion that shouldn't have changed everything.

But it had.

He'd given her everything she'd ever wanted, but she'd known from the beginning it wouldn't last. This wasn't her home, it was his. And this wasn't her life. She was nothing here...nothing but his. She couldn't fault him for taking it away. No, it was much easier to shake her fist at the prover-bial sky. Jax might be temporary, but too many pieces of her hadn't gotten the memo.

She'd fallen. Hard.

It felt way too much like a high school crush, where something as small as a passing glance turned into initials sketched into hearts and whispers of forever. No grown woman should entertain such thoughts—especially in the face of knowing she had less than twenty-four hours to ever see him again—but somewhere in the dark he'd touched more than her body. They'd forged a connection that went so far beyond physical that the thought of losing it crippled her. But it wasn't right. Couldn't be. It didn't matter that she'd never felt as close to another human being as she had him. It only mattered that in a matter of hours they'd be through.

Done.

Over.

Who was she kidding? After his exit, they probably already were.

I'm sorry if that's not good enough, Colorado, but it's all I've got.

She wondered if he had second thoughts. About taking her to the park. Going back to her room. Stealing her from Focker.

Telling her he'd give her back.

What a joke.

She wanted to tell him she wasn't his to give, but she'd be his for a long time to come. She had quite a few mountains to climb to get past that, and she strongly suspected every clear blue sky she ever saw would be his. Every sunset. Every flaming red rock. Every dream, every memory. He'd changed it all.

She wouldn't change that. Maybe the outcome—she wished they had more time—but what they had wasn't meant to be anything more. She didn't want to cling to him only to have things fall apart. She'd take what he'd given her and treasure it, and that would have to be enough.

After spending a disproportionate amount of her time— and budget—in Hershey's Chocolate World, she headed back to the hotel and prayed she'd still fit in her ball gown. Between the breakfast Jax had sent Friday morning, the all-you-can-eat buffet, and the chocolate she'd just consumed, she'd be lucky if she didn't need to call room service for help getting the zipper up. Managing to do so on her own only left her paranoid the stupid thing would split, but she'd take her chances.

One more night in Vegas.

But it wasn't the same. Couldn't be.

She still had an hour before the ball, so she went to the hotel casino, only a little self-conscious to do so in a formal gown. Her short tenure in the city had quickly taught her two things. One, anything goes. Two, "anything" didn't cause most people to look twice. Sure enough, she found herself at the bar with a man who appeared to be wearing a bikini top and a woman wearing a French maid costume. As far as she could tell, no one paid more than passing attention to either one of them.

The bartender was on her in a second. "What'll you have?"

Ellie blinked, stupidly surprised anyone would ask. She didn't have a clue what to order, so she nodded toward the concoction in front of the French maid. "Um, one of those."

"Blue Hawaii, coming up."

Well, alrighty then. She watched him mix the drink and still had no idea what went in it, but if she didn't hate it and it didn't put her on the floor, at least she had a go-to for the next time. As if there'd be one.

She didn't have the chance to pay for the drink before a man slid onto the seat next to her and shoved a twenty across the bar.

"She's on me," he said.

In your dreams. The guy was attractive enough, though he'd gone a little overboard with hair product. Ellie wasn't high maintenance, and as a rule she wasn't into guys who would require more time at the bathroom mirror than she. Or those who weren't Jax.

She'd get over that last part eventually. She'd have to.

"Where you from, gorgeous?"

"Colorado."

The response hadn't been hers. It was Jax, and if looks could kill, High Maintenance Man would have disintegrated on the spot.

"She's not available," Jax said. "Beat it."

The other man gave a cocky, half-drunk smile. "I was here first, and I paid for the drink."

Jax glanced at her glass, then extracted a bill from his pocket and planted it against the other man's chest with enough force to make him stumble backward. "She's not for sale, jackass."

The offender grabbed for the cash then spread his arms in surrender, backing across the floor to nearly collide with a waitress carrying a tray full of cocktails. He spun out of her way, flashed a smile, and disappeared into the crowd.

"What was that?" Jax asked, his voice meticulously even.

"Unwanted attention."

He eyed her appreciatively, although he didn't seem too happy about it. "I'm not surprised, in that dress. I should have come with a baseball bat."

"Thank you. I think."

He sat on the seat next to hers. "I'm sorry I ran out this morning."

"I understand you have a job to do," she said. As if she believed it was his job that had him backpedaling out of her bed. Her life.

"It's not that."

Her gaze drifted from his face to his biceps where his tattoo peeked from under his shirt sleeve. For the first time, she noticed letters carefully, beautifully woven into the design. *G-R-A*. She pushed up his sleeve with a fingertip to see the rest. *C-I-E*. When she looked up at him, his eyes were on her.

"My sister," he said. "Gracie was my sister."

"What happened?" she asked softly. She hadn't dared

to ask the first time he'd mentioned her, but she and Jax had shared so much since then.

"I was sixteen. She was twelve. We were on vacation in the mountains. *Your* mountains." He paused and took a break that shook him, but he didn't meet her eye. "She loved to ski. We were due to fly home that day, and I let her talk me into one more run. She was supposed to stay on the intermediate slope unless our parents were with her, but she took the black diamond. At the time I was good, but I wasn't the skier she was. I didn't have any business on an expert trail, but I couldn't just let her go, you know?"

Ellie nodded. Already, her eyes were hot with unshed tears. It didn't matter how many years had passed—the parallels between Ellie's job and the way he'd lost his sister had to shake him. They'd shake anybody.

"The sun was warm on that side of the mountain," he said. "They hadn't closed it, so she insisted it would be fine. I should have stopped her, but she was ahead of me. There were signs against it, but she went off the trail."

"On purpose?"

"I think so. It was a deliberate turn, just like the trail head. Other skiers had gone before her. You could see the tracks. She wanted to try it. She'd asked all day, but I always pointed to the signs. I never said, 'Hey, might be dangerous.' Just, 'There's a sign, so don't.'" He tapped restlessly on the bar. Had to wave away the bartender. "She wasn't out of control," he finally said. "That was me. I think that's been me ever since. I just stood there watching that damned red hat of hers weave through the snow, then she was gone."

"A crevasse?" The deep cracks through ice were hard to see under fresh snow, and they were dangerous. A fall into one could be deadly—one of many reasons skiing out of designated areas was forbidden.

"No. Avalanche."

"Oh, God, Jax. I'm so sorry."

"I tore down that black diamond trail to get help, but by the time they found her, it was too late. I should have followed her. I should have been there with her."

"If she was good enough to take an expert trail, she knew better than to ski out of bounds. It's not your fault."

"Tell that to my parents. They didn't care that she'd gone off on her own, or that I managed to stress fracture *both* of my legs going down that mountain after help. It was my fault because I told her she could take one more run." He looked down at his hands, picking at an invisible spot on the bar. "It was sixteen years ago, and those were the last words they said to me."

"I'm so sorry," she said again. "But they're wrong, Jax."

He shrugged. "Doesn't matter. I made the wrong decision that day. I guess they're entitled to do the same."

Anger elbowed through her sorrow. "It wasn't your fault. You were a kid, and they forced onto you a burden an adult couldn't handle, let alone a child."

"Doesn't matter," he repeated. "I just wanted you to know…to know why."

"Why what?"

"I care about you, and the minute I realized that, I should have walked away. I certainly shouldn't have spent the night with you, Ellie, because you deserve more than what I have to give."

She caught her lip between her teeth. He'd called her by her name. Not Colorado, but Ellie. And it hurt.

"You're wrong," she said.

A short, dark laugh escaped him. "You're a fucking ski instructor. It should have been over right then and there."

She winced. Under the circumstances, he was probably right. "But it wasn't."

"Because I'm a selfish bastard." He turned his head, scrubbing with his hand the stubble that darkened his chin. "Because you're the sun. You're the goddamn sun, and it's been so long since I've been warm."

Her heart broke, every piece into a million more. He wasn't running.

He was already gone.

He hadn't backpedaled because he didn't want her. He did it because he wanted her too much.

"What does that tell you?" she asked. "That I made you warm?"

He met her gaze evenly. "That you're too good for me. Too good to get caught up in this. Dammit, this is too much for two days."

Two days. She felt like she'd known him forever. "You've been unhappy half your life. You don't have to forget, but you have to live."

He stopped short of answering her when yelling erupted from a nearby bank of slot machines. At first she thought someone must have hit a jackpot, but the harsh tones quickly suggested otherwise. "What—?"

"Get to the other side of the bar." He pointed across the free-standing station to an area that put the bulk of the bar between her and the commotion. "Now."

She grabbed her drink—interesting choice of priorities for someone who didn't know enough to name a single one—

and moved as he sprinted in the direction of the yelling. She tried to make out what was being said, but despite the hush around her, the general casino noise managed to drown out the details. Ellie stood on tiptoes, unable to see anything but the throng of onlookers and the attempt of a pair of hotel security personnel to break through. Then a man burst from the group and ran right for her.

Standing perched on her tiptoes in an evening gown didn't make for good reaction time. He caught her elbow as he plowed past, forcing Ellie hard against the bar. She managed a few choice words as her drink sloshed onto her dress, but it was over before she realized what happened. Several strides away, the guy was grabbed by security.

Jax walked from the rapidly dispersing crowd, holding the elbow of an elderly, slightly bent woman who, with a gray bun and an old handbag, looked every bit the part of the granny who owned Tweety Bird. She ranted about a man trying to steal her winnings, and Jax looked on with sympathy…until he saw Ellie. His eyes flashed dark. Fierce. He didn't abandon the woman, but he appeared to hurry her along until she caught sight of the man who had jostled Ellie, at which point the old woman left Jax in the dust. She was a spry little thing in her orthopedic shoes, and even more so when she got close enough to whack her target with her purse. The security guards traded barely-suppressed grins and made only halfhearted attempts to shield the perp while she beat the crap out of him with her bag—one of those old-school numbers with actual corners.

Ellie watched with a grin on her face. And Blue Hawaii on her chest.

"Are you okay?" Jax didn't smile. He didn't look the

least bit amused by any of it.

"I'm fine. He just bumped me."

"Are you sure?" Worry penetrated the dazzling blue of his eyes.

Buoyed her. "You do care."

"I never said I didn't care. Just that I couldn't."

"Jax—"

"Look, I get it, okay? I won't deny what's between us, but I can't accept it. I told you about Gracie so you'd understand. I want to be the man I was last night. I want nothing more than to be him for you, but I can't, and there's nothing to be gained by pretending."

"Were you pretending last night?"

After a long, bitter silence in which the entire casino seemed to still around them, he spoke. "You said yourself, nothing here is real. You and climbing mountains and hiding here, that's me. And I can't give that away. Not to a woman like you who deserves the moon and the stars." A short, humorless laugh followed. "I can't even see the damned stars from here."

"But you know where they are," she insisted. "And you go there so often to seek them that they know you at the gate. Don't tell me you're broken, Jax. Don't tell me you're too broken when you still care enough to look."

He shook his head. Slow, deliberate. "Not anymore."

"What does that mean?"

"I've found it. I've found what I've looked for, and I can't have it. And I know that now. It's over. It has to be." Blue eyes pierced her brown ones. Said good-bye. "Later, Colorado. At the ball. You can meet up with Focker one more time, and then we'll be done."

Chapter Ten

Ellie spent a few minutes in the ladies room attempting to spot clean her dress, but mostly remembering the moment she'd watched her ticket disappear down the toilet and thought her life was over. Now she felt as if it had begun, if not with that moment, than the one where she'd walked into Jax. *Wolverine*. It fit the exterior, but no one would ever guess the tenderness under that surface. She smiled at herself in the mirror. Thought of how he'd smiled.

Of how he said it had been too long.

And she was furious.

Was this what it was like when you didn't wait for everything to be right? What irony. Things with her ex had never felt like this. She hadn't realized it, having nothing to compare it to, but there must have been something in the back of her mind that told her things weren't right. That she shouldn't have to fight to label and compartmentalize. If she hadn't realized that, she would have been much more devastated when she caught him with another woman. She'd been upset, for sure, but in retrospect it was more about her plans falling apart than in the betrayal. There hadn't been anything there to begin with. They were held together—at least on paper—by her rules.

Jax blew rules all to hell.

A person didn't pencil "Have orgasm in a public park" onto one's schedule. No one scheduled syrup. In no datebook ever, electronic or otherwise, had anyone ever written, "Put on his shirt so he can tear it off and devour you."

Jax Mathis had changed everything.

Shaking her head, she gave up on the Blue Hawaii. The spot was hardly noticeable under the harsh fluorescent glare, so it would be invisible under the ballroom lights—assuming, that was, that they resembled all the fictional ones she'd seen on television.

She'd never been to a ball.

You can meet up with Focker one more time, and then we'll be done.

The words irked her beyond reason. It didn't matter how far she'd fallen. He'd made it clear he wouldn't be there to catch her, but if he thought he was going to hand her over to another man, he had another think coming. She withdrew her phone from her clutch and checked the time. Only about fifteen minutes until the ball started. She had a text from Taylor. A reminder.

What happens in Vegas gets told to the bestie, pronto. And your dog ate my shoe.

Ellie tapped back a reply. Her new mantra.

*I suck at one-night stands. And your next pair of
shoes is on me.*

Taylor would lose her mind. Ellie grinned at the thought,
then set her notifications to vibrate and dropped her phone
in her purse.

The ballroom was on the second floor. Ellie opted to
take the escalator. On the ride up, she noticed the purse-
packing granny back at the slots, glasses perched at the end
of her nose and a drink in her hand. Ellie wished she could
put the pieces back together so easily. Move on like nothing had happened. A cloak of melancholy settled over her.
It was her last night in Vegas, and she would spend it with
a room full of strangers. Them and one man who wanted to
take it all back and pretend that was all they'd ever been.

The second floor was clogged with ball attendees in formal wear, a sea of black tuxes and a myriad of gowns that
somehow complemented the Masquerade's color scape of
gold, purple, green, red, and silver. But if those colors were
considered matching, clashing would be more of a challenge
than not.

Just inside the ballroom, a regal woman with a gorgeous
light blue floor-length gown—one presumably not doused in
Blue Hawaii—greeted guests, introducing herself as Patricia
Plimpton. To Ellie, she said, "You'll have some punch, won't
you, dear?"

A good stiff drink sounded better, but Ellie nodded
anyway.

Patricia patted her on the shoulder and leaned close.
"You don't look happy. Have two glasses. Perhaps even a
third. It'll do wonders for you."

Ellie blinked, bewildered, but the hostess was quickly swallowed by revelers.

And then she was alone. At a ball.

She dutifully took a glass of punch and meandered the room's periphery, scanning for Jax. She found Focker first. Instinctively, she expected the once-familiar thrill of seeing him on a book cover to shoot through her, tenfold because he was in the flesh—albeit less flesh than their previous encounter in which he'd been shirtless. But nothing. Absolutely nothing.

Focker didn't look at anyone in particular, not even when they appeared to speak to him. Rather he continuously searched the room, fiddling alternatively with his cuffs and his hair. Despite his frequent ministrations, not a strand fell out of place. The angle of the light hitting his face suggested the skin there was as baby soft as his hands had been on her arms for the photo shoot—no rough edges like Jax's.

She shivered, still feeling the thrill of the abrasion between her thighs. Of what his tongue had done to her.

"I guess he's still got it."

She didn't even turn to look at Jax, though she briefly entertained the thought of grinding her spiked heel into his foot. "He doesn't look happy to be here."

"You wouldn't either if someone said you'd leave in a body bag."

She swiveled to look at him. "Are you serious?"

"Dead."

"Funny."

"Same threats he's gotten all week, none of which have led to anything even remotely worrisome. He's got a half dozen suits on his payroll in here, and as much as I know he wouldn't want to admit it, he's sweating."

"Is that why he looks like that?"

"Like what? Devastatingly handsome?" Jax said the words with boredom, as if he'd heard them a thousand times, and she hated that a version had once come from her.

"Like he'd rather be anywhere else."

"Hard to blame him under the circumstances," Jax said, "but he needs to up his game if he doesn't want to piss off all those women." He shot her a sideways glance. "He's supposed to make each one feel like she's the only one in the room. That's what his manager tells him before every event."

"That's what they all want, isn't it?"

He gave her a hard look. "I guess you'd know."

Ouch. "That isn't fair."

"Maybe not. But it's true. If it weren't true, you wouldn't know my name."

Ellie took a breath and did her best not to show it. "Is this you trying to drive a wedge between us because you're afraid of how you feel about me, because things aren't as over as you seem to want to think they are? Or is this you being jealous?"

He didn't answer.

"I get it. It's both. Well, guess what, jackass. I haven't wanted him since the moment I set eyes on you. You can take it, leave it, or run from it. What you do with that is your choice, but don't you *dare* lay it on me."

"I'll keep that in mind," he said, casually, like he'd just offered to get her a drink. "I'll catch up with you in a few."

She stared daggers at his back as he walked away. She wanted to go after and *dare* him to look her in the eye and *tell her*, dammit, that he didn't care, but to what end? He'd already admitted he cared. What good would it do either of them to dwell on it? None of this was meant to last. She'd go back home to Minturn knowing for the first time what it felt like to be needed, and she'd feel the void more than she ever had. And he'd stay there, living in the damned desert, all the while insisting he didn't need the sun.

Whatever.

She all but stomped over to the punch bowl and got a refill. A man asked her to dance. She declined, then had immediate second thoughts. Jax hadn't been happy with the guy buying her a drink downstairs, so maybe if he saw her with someone else…

Nope.

She wasn't playing games. Vegas would always be his. She didn't want any other memories to crowd that out. And she didn't want to hurt him. Despite what he claimed about their nonexistence as a thing, she didn't want him thinking for one second that she thought she could move on. She had no idea what his memories would hold, but one thing was for sure—he'd look back and see her in *his* arms, not someone else's. And so would she.

The punch disappeared. She went for a third. She'd have to slow down, if for no other reason than she'd spend half the night in line for the ladies room. Ball gowns, even like hers of the soft, flowing variety, didn't exactly mesh with bathroom stalls.

Her determination not to be anyone's but his landed her on wallflower duty, but that was okay. The event, like the rest of Sin City, was surreal. She recognized a number of other cover models, which surprised her. If she knew faces other than Focker's, her singular attraction hadn't been as singular

as she'd thought it, but it didn't matter now. What she wanted couldn't be found on the cover of a book.

Nearby, a group of women fangirled an author who
looked bewildered by their shrieks. They made a small scene,
drawing some attention. Ellie sidestepped them, her gaze
automatically skating the room for Jax. When she found him
again, her heart skipped a beat, then tumbled down a flight
of stairs. He definitely wore a tux that night. The fact that he
periodically tugged at his collar only made him impossibly
more adorable. He was all broad shoulders and blue eyes, his
short dark hair still tousled. She remembered running her
fingers through it, holding on for dear life while he changed
everything she thought she knew about sex. She felt impossibly privileged that he'd shared himself with her.

Would the wanting ever stop?

She waved off a waiter with a tray full of fluted glasses.
The punch had her a bit lightheaded. It was supposed to be
non-alcoholic. Had to be the sugar. It and Hershey's World
had provided most of her sustenance for the day, so it was
no small wonder she was upright. Instinctively, she searched
the room for Jax. She found him near the corner Focker had
apparently adopted, for she hadn't seen him anywhere else
all night. She thought of the threats Jax mentioned and wondered if Focker felt safer in the corner.

Or if he had before whatever was going on over there
had started happening.

She watched as Jax edged between Pretty Boy and a red-
faced man who gestured wildly. One of those angry husbands
he'd mentioned? Focker had turned white as a sheet, and Jax
was pushing the other guy toward the exit. Subtle enough
not to draw a bunch of attention, but leaving no question

that homeboy was out. Uniformed hotel security waited near the door and took over for Jax. Relief sliced through the tension in her shoulders. Jax met her eyes briefly, then looked away.

She just stood there, aching. Thinking she should leave. What if he thought she was waiting for him to bring her to Focker? She'd probably never get the chance to tell him otherwise, and she didn't want him thinking it.

No, no, no.

She needed to get out of there. Maybe have a steak. Filets came wrapped in bacon, didn't they? Yep, that was it. She'd go find a place that served a mean bacon-wrapped filet mignon and she'd sip water until her head stopped spinning. Then she'd go back to her room and stay there until she had to head to the airport.

Done. Deal.

She deposited the punch glass on a tray of empties and turned for the exit. No good-bye. No chance he'd think she was hanging on. Just…done.

Almost to the exit, she was plowed down for the second time that day. She stumbled out of the way, backstepping several paces, managing with the help of a stranger to find her footing before she fell. Then she realized who had hit her.

It was the man Jax had escorted out, and he was headed straight for Pretty Boy's corner.

She saw Jax's gaze register on the intruder. Saw the moment he got pissed. Saw, as the man moved away from her at an angle, that he held a gun.

Oh, God, no.

The scene played out in stop motion. The man holding

the firearm. Focker diving behind a table. And Jax, that son of a bitch, going straight for the weapon. The attacker's eyes…Ellie didn't think she'd ever forget the rage there the moment his gaze shifted from Focker to Jax. Behind Jax, security quietly cleared the immediate area, and she remembered wondering what the point was. Would the gun only shoot straight? Would a bullet not travel the distance of the ballroom? And then she realized the bullet would have to go through Jax. They all knew it. They all *expected* it, and they just stood there, a bunch of bastards in the odd sea of calm where most of the guests didn't seem to realize anything was amiss.

Jax. His name stuck in her throat. Tried to claw its way out, but screaming would only distract him so she bit back, forced back the tears already fighting to fall. She waited in terror for the blast of gunfire. Worried the guy had already pulled the trigger under guise of a silencer and Jax's motions were all momentum. *No blood.* There was no blood.

In an instant, slow motion morphed into crippling speed. Jax flew, slamming into the man, twisting his arm toward the ceiling in one blunt motion that sent them both sailing. The assailant hit the floor, and Jax landed on top of him. One blow to the man's arm and Jax had the gun. By the time she realized what happened, he'd pulled something out of the weapon and handed the pieces to one of the other security personnel, then sat there on the intruder's chest. Breathing hard, but otherwise outwardly unfettered. Like it was nothing.

Like he hadn't run up to a gun that had been pointed at his chest.

His eyes met hers. People rushed around him, and for a

moment he was gone. Then someone dragged the gunman to his feet, and the crowd of security personnel rushed past him, leaving Jax standing there. Alone.

Which, one way or another, had been his game plan all along.

He'd told her as much, but the bitter, terrifying truth was something she couldn't unsee. Tears spilled over, and she turned away. She heard him call after her, but there was no going back.

"Colorado." He caught up to her, grabbed her arm.

She looked down at the offending touch, then at him. Saying nothing.

He dropped her arm, but not her gaze. "We need to talk. Let me go clear it with security. I'm sure I'll have to answer questions, but everything is on surveillance footage. Just… will you wait?"

She nodded. Hadn't meant to, but it happened.

He wiped a tear off her cheek with his thumb. "Wait for me."

She nodded again, then watched him walk away. The next day it would be her leaving. Over was over. What difference did it make? Sad, confused, and tear-stained, she turned her back on him and visited the ladies room. There was no salvaging what little makeup she wore, so she washed her face and started over, then headed back to wait for Jax.

She felt like what she'd witnessed had been down a rabbit hole, and now she had to blink her way back out. Surprisingly little fuss had been made of the incident. Surely the news spread like wildfire, but there was already nothing to see. Rumors were equally inflated—*a mob hit*—and dismissed—*publicity stunt*—and the revelers continued on with their party. She didn't even try to be a part of it. She just waited for Jax. An hour passed, after which she was asked by the police to answer a few questions. She found they were set up in another conference room, where there was no trace of Jax. She recounted what she'd seen, then left her contact information. When she exited the interview, she found him standing in the corridor.

"I'm sorry you got wrapped up in that," he said. Not like a lover, like a man who had worshipped every inch of her body, but like he felt obligated. Polite. Stilted. Like he hadn't almost fucking *died*.

Her emotional dam, which by that point rivaled the Hoover holding back the Colorado, burst. If she had a downstream, everything in its path would have been obliterated. "That's it? *That's* what you're sorry for?"

Her voice hit a volume that had people looking their way. Jax took her arm and led her down the hall and around a corner. "Yes," he said. "You could have gotten hurt."

Anger flared, then exploded. "What about you?" she yelled. "Damn you, Jax. You're not expendable. Do you get that? You don't get to just *die* because you think no one cares."

"I get to do my job," he said evenly, "because that's what I'm paid to do."

"No one is paying you to die. You don't even like him, but you're willing to die for him!"

"You're right."

She counted to five. Then ten. She bit back the anger. The fear. The whatever-it-was that had her chest in a fevered, achy knot. "How long are you going to punish yourself for something that happened sixteen years ago?"

"This has nothing to do with that," he said evenly.

"It has *everything* do to with that," she shot back. "You think everyone is worth saving but you, and you're wrong. If anything had happened to you—"

"Then what? You'd be on that plane tomorrow either way, so what difference does it make?"

She stared at him, stunned. "You think I don't care? You're the one pushing. You are the one so damned determined not to care about anyone that you won't see what's in front of your face. And I'm done, Jax. I'm done fighting for something you so obviously don't want."

She spun to leave, but he caught her. His features were tight. Tense. "You don't know what you're talking about."

She stood there, chest heaving. Tears threatening. Her entire world tipping and spinning on what he'd say next. "Then say it. *Admit it.*"

He let her go, and her heart sank. Shattered. She turned to go, but his soft words stopped her in her tracks.

"I want you."

She turned. Stared at the man who had become such a part of her she no longer recognized who she'd been before him. Wondered if she'd only imagined those words on his lips.

"I want you," he said again. Louder. Bitter. "You fucking come in here, and you're everything I thought I couldn't have. You're the sun in the damned sky. and I don't know what I'm going to do when you're gone. Is that what you wanted to hear?"

"Is it the truth?" He voice shook. Her body shook.

With tension threading his limbs and his eyes flashing blue sparks, Jax looked like he could pulverize granite. "Yes, it's the goddamn truth."

"Then stop fighting it," she whispered.

A moment passed. Then another. The distant sounds from the ballroom faded, and all that was left was the thud of her heart in her ears and the jagged edge of his breath.

Then his mouth was on hers. Passion tore through the kiss. Tore through *her*, and then she was against the wall. He cupped her breast, toying with her nipple through the fabric. Then pinching, and when she gasped he deepened the kiss. Needing the heat of his skin, she fumbled blindly with his shirt, only to have him release her and rip free the fasteners. Buttons popped and danced erratic circles in the periphery, bubbly like champagne.

"Your shirt."

"Don't care." He reached down and slid his hands up her legs, dragging her gown to her thighs. Then he lifted her, once again trapping her against the wall. This time his mouth aligned with her breast, and he snatched the offending fabric, freeing her to the heat of his tongue.

If he hadn't held her, she would have hit the ground. The rough licking, softness of his lips, and bite of his teeth had her spiraling. She tightened her legs around him, her body begging for the sweet relief of pressure, *any* pressure, against her clit. He responded instantly, dragging his hand from her ass to push his fingers inside her.

"Fuck, you're drenched."

She wriggled against his hand, desperately seeking contact, but he withheld. Probably on purpose, the jackass. *"Now."*

One word. One demand. When he withdrew she almost hit him with her small clutch, which she inexplicably still held, but then she realized he was fumbling with his zipper. The seconds until he freed himself felt like an eternity, but then he'd pushed aside her thong and he was inside her, hot and thick and filling her with a pressure that bordered on pain. She almost came on the spot.

Oh, shit, oh, shit, oh, shit.

He gave a moment's pause—not long enough for any civilized person to adapt to his size—then withdrew and came back with so much force the wall rattled at her back.

"Do it again," she managed.

He rolled his hips back until nearly free of her, then slammed back, thrusting deep. And this time he didn't stop. She was helpless to do anything but hold on as he fucked her hard. Against a wall. Just around the corner from a very busy corridor.

Orgasm tore through her with ruthless speed. He must have felt it, must have been waiting for it, for mere seconds after the first ripple shuddered through her he muttered a string of obscenities and changed his pace from long strokes to short stuttered bursts. The motion had him rocking against her clit, had her seeing stars. Another bigger, brighter explosion rocked her, a dizzying combination of exquisite pressure and burning heat, as he landed hard against her. His cock pumped without him, driving against her G spot as he ground his pelvis lightly against her.

Oh, sweet Jesus.

She didn't know where one orgasm stopped and the next began. Only that all that punishing force had disseminated into sweet mercy, and it wasn't enough.

Nowhere near enough.

He eased out of her body, then steadied her as she

attempted to find her feet. She straightened her gown as he tried to fit back in his pants. She giggled.

He caught her when she swayed. "What the hell. Are you okay? You haven't been drinking, have you? Because if that happened—"

"It definitely happened." She was dizzy. Hot and aching. Needy. She had one night left, and spending it without him wasn't an option. "Take me upstairs, Jax. Take me up there now so it can happen again."

Chapter Eleven

Well, hell. Jax stood there on the verge of dropping to his knees to beg Ellie's forgiveness for not using protection, and she was demanding more. Maybe she hadn't realized what happened. If so, that was the biggest neon sign in the city that he shouldn't take her upstairs, but there wasn't much point. He'd make damn sure he didn't forget a second time, and there wasn't taking back what already happened. He was clean—he knew that for a fact—and if there were any other consequences…well, they'd deal with that later. Twelve hours wouldn't make a difference.

He held her hand on the way to the elevator, and as soon as the door slid shut he pulled her into his arms. Kissed her. Tasted everything. She was soft, molded to him, and well and truly his. No idea what the hell he was going to do about that, other than spend the night making sure she knew he cared. He never meant for that to be a question, but he had a feeling she wouldn't accept where they were headed.

Separate ways.

It hurt. Crushed him that she'd be gone. But the burn would have to fuel him, because there was no way on this earth he deserved this woman. He'd already proven, again, that he couldn't protect her. And she'd made it clear she'd never forgive him for doing his job.

Just a job.

Not a life.

Not Ellie.

His eyes stung, and his throat tightened. It was like the pain of losing Gracie, only this time he wasn't watching someone go.

This time he was pushing.

But not yet, dammit. *Not yet.*

He wound his fingers through her hair and slanted his head, deepening the kiss. She moaned, the sweet vibration rocking him to his core. By the time the elevator doors slid open on her floor, he was rock hard. He walked her backward down the hall, kissing her, both of them stumbling then landing solidly against her door. Just like they'd been downstairs, when he'd been buried in her, nothing between them but heat. He'd never, ever had sex without a condom. Had no idea it could feel like that. But it wouldn't with just anyone. Couldn't.

It had to be her.

She managed to wrangle her key card from her little purse. He took it without looking, trying and failing three or four times before the door finally unlocked. They fell through, and he dug the condom out of his pocket. That he'd put it there made him wince. What had he been planning? To hand her over to Focker and throw in the rubber as a parting gift?

This, dumbass. You wanted this. Because if Focker had fucking touched Ellie, Jax would have torn him apart with his bare hands.

She wasn't making fast enough progress shedding her dress, so he helped. Stripped her in one swoop, leaving her standing there in her heels and thong, the latter not quite back to rights after their encounter in the corridor.

Oh. Fuck. Yes.

"You're beautiful," he said. He scooped her so she straddled him, riding him backward to the bed. Tossed her down, then proceeded to kiss and lick his way down to her thong, taking a long, languid detour around each breast. The more she moaned and grabbed at his hair, the more he slowed. He liked feeling her squirm. Liked the way she begged without a word. He took her thong off with his teeth. Fucked her with his tongue in the process, and she liked it so much he feasted. Probably wouldn't have guessed he'd enjoy the taste so much, knowing half of what left her so wet her had been him, but the intimacy got to him.

It got to him a little too much. He pulled back and made a halfhearted attempt to wipe his face, then tore into the condom. One of the giant ribbons hanging off the hotel caught his eye through the window. God, this place. This woman.

He didn't even bother undressing all the way. Just tossed the rented jacket and the ruined shirt aside, kicked off his shoes, and opened his fly. Once the condom was on, he crawled on top of her to find her grinning.

"What?"

"You're smiling."

He took the accusation in stride. "I told you, Colorado.

Only you."

"I like being that person."

"I like it too." And that was dangerous. Fortunately, he had a hell of a distraction. He caught the back of her knees and lifted her legs, settling between them with her ankles thrown over his shoulders. "Nice stripper heels."

She gasped as he pushed inside her, but despite the gouges she'd just left on his arms, she grinned. "You have a weird thing about noticing shoes. And I am *so* not a stripper."

"Good. Because I hate to think I'd have to share you with…anyone."

"Not ever," she said.

The words meant something to him. Something he didn't care to think too much about, and probably couldn't if he tried. Not buried balls deep in a hot, tight slice of heaven. He rolled against her, just enjoying the sensation. Knowing if he dropped her legs and pounded into her like he wanted, he'd be toast in seconds. Maybe less.

Been there, done that. But not nearly enough.

She was losing it. He wondered if she'd even come in the hall, or if all that shaking had been him. He was pretty sure she had, but he'd have to make it up to her just in case. She was definitely headed in the right direction. Every time he leaned forward and increased the pressure on her clit, her grip on the bed tightened. He loosened his hold on her legs, allowing them to widen around him, and he changed the angle, pushing deeper, grinding harder.

"Oh. My. God."

Her hips jerked. He leaned in, letting her legs fall aside. Found her clit with his thumb and her mouth with his tongue. Tasted her, swallowed her cries as she fell apart. He managed to hang on until she'd stopped pulsing around him, then he let go. After what she'd done to him in the corridor, he was surprised he had anything left to give, but he didn't think he'd ever stop. Didn't think he wanted to.

Their kisses grew languid. Teasing. He eased out of her, then rolled to the side and drew her into his arms. "Two quickies in a combined five minutes, plus the one yesterday. Either we're really good at this or really bad."

She smiled. Lit the room. "You're amazing at this."

"Not so amazing," he said. "More of a victim of whatever you've done to me."

"Can you stay?" she asked softly. "Just the night. I won't ask anything more."

"I might have to deal with the police."

"But until you do?"

"I'll stay," he said. *Some sacrifice.* "Just let me go take care of this mess."

She smiled through passion-drenched, half-lidded eyes.

God, he was screwed.

He went to her bathroom and tossed the condom. Noticed a bra and a pair of underwear hanging on the towel rack. The latter garment was covered with little yellow flowers. Didn't look much like her. Didn't matter. He preferred her naked.

Naked and his.

When he went back in the room she had the room service menu open. "Do they have filet here?"

"Filet of…?"

"Mignon. With the bacon."

He shook his head, failing to dislodge the laugh that threatened escape. "There's a place down the strip with the best I've ever had. I can call."

"I'd kind of rather stay here," she said.

His gaze caroused the curves and soft planes of her body. Yeah, he could get behind that plan. "I was going to say we'd order in."

Her eyes widened. "They deliver?"

"I know the chef."

"In that case, make it happen."

He patted his pocket. Found his cell. Was surprised it survived the ride. He'd have to up his game a little. "Wine?"

"None for me, but help yourself."

He placed his call. Got an ear full of shit about trying to turn fine dining into fast food. Told the chef almighty to take his time and it wouldn't *be* fast. The chef hung up on him, muttering something in French Jax didn't understand. A couple of minutes later, he got a bill via email. He paid double for a tip, then tossed the phone aside.

Ellie sat all twisted in a sheet, watching him. "Just like that?"

"It'll be a little while."

She melted into a grin. "However will we pass the time?"

There was always that whole *on his knees and begging for forgiveness* thing. He hated that she might not have realized it yet. Maybe she was on birth control. Maybe she trusted he was clean and didn't need him to say it, but that bugged him too. He hadn't earned that kind of trust. He wasn't ready for it. He didn't need it. He'd be gone by morning, and so would she.

"Not with another quickie," he said. "The next time I make love to you, it's going to last all night."

She stared at him, bewildered. Frozen.

What the hell had he... Oh, shit. He'd never uttered

those words in his life. Some people threw them around generically, but not him.

And she was looking at him like she knew it.

He picked up his ruined shirt and tossed it to her. So much for naked. He still preferred it, but naked presented its own problems.

She caught it. Studied it. "Getting tired of the view?"

"No, baby. But if you stay like that, that headboard is going to be hitting the wall too hard for us to hear the door when the steak arrives."

She relaxed into a grin. Tugged on his shirt. Couldn't help the ruined buttons.

He took her hand. Spun her like they were dancing, only dancing wasn't a thing he did. He held her there anyway, the two of them swaying to music that didn't exist. Her hair fell in soft waves, tickling his nose. The room was as dark as could be with the city glowing through the open drapes, but he saw her. He saw everything.

Everything but tomorrow without her in it.

All the more reason to make it happen.

He pulled her closer, body to body, flesh to flesh. The shirt hadn't done its job. The tantalizing swath of exposed skin included a partial view of full breasts. Tight nipples. A mark he'd left. He wanted to dive right in and leave another one, but he settled for having her fully in his arms. And holding her like that made him realize he didn't hug people, either. He didn't hug. Didn't dance. Didn't make love.

Didn't die.

He'd yet to process what happened in the ballroom. He faced relatively few confrontations. Most had been with women, none of whom had been packing more than an irrational idea that laying eyes—or hands—on a celebrity would somehow make her life complete. The loaded weapon in a room full of hundreds of people had been a new thing. Despite his happenstance entry into the field of personal security, he'd subsequently trained for the job. He knew weapons. Could kick ass in hand-to-hand combat. Didn't think twice about lunging for the guy with the gun, but in the back of his mind he hadn't seen his client or the ballroom full of people.

He'd seen Ellie.

Couldn't stop.

He'd never escape her scent. Never forget her taste or the sweet slide of her body against his.

Never wanted to.

Had to.

He loosened his hold, only to find himself staring into sweet, questioning eyes. They fluttered closed when he kissed her. The urge to ease her onto the bed was strong, but he hadn't been kidding when he said they wouldn't hear the food arrive. So he kept his tour of her mouth light, despite the way his heart pounded and body demanded more.

"You think you'll think of me next time you play the slots?" she asked.

"I don't play the slots," he said. "But to answer your question, I won't ever see another one and not think of you."

Another slot machine. Another sunset. Another anything. He'd think of her forever. This thing between them didn't have a chance in hell, but it had one more night.

And not a damned minute more.

• • •

After an incredible dinner, Ellie almost felt normal again. If, that was, normal could even be a thing with tall, dark, and sexy sharing her room. Her bed. She couldn't stop thinking about what he'd done the night before. She still couldn't believe she'd told him about her ex, but what was even more unbelievable was his reaction. Whatever second thoughts had him leaving that morning and trying to hand her over to Focker in the afternoon had clearly taken a backseat to... what? She wasn't sure what he'd done. Or maybe she was just afraid to admit to herself, but there wasn't much point in holding on to the denial.

He'd said it.

Next time I make love to you.

After they'd eaten, she'd excused herself to brush her teeth. When she returned, he stood at one of the large windows, his gaze trained over the city crawling far below.

"What do you see out there?" she asked.

"Possibilities."

The answer surprised her. "What about in here?"

He turned from the window. His appraisal ate her alive. "You scare me, Colorado."

"I know," she said softly. "I like that part."

"I see something I'm not ready to see," he admitted.

"I like that even better."

He touched her face. Pushed back her hair. "I can't, baby. I can't do it."

She'd known that, but the words didn't hurt any less. "I hope you're not talking about tonight."

He broke into a grin. "I can definitely do it tonight."

"Then let's forget what happens after." Twenty four hours from then, she'd be back home in Minturn with no expectations that her memories could do this man justice. She needed this now. Needed him. "Let's just have tonight. I'm okay with that."

"I hope *okay* is an understatement." He gently pushed his shirt from her shoulders, his gaze following it as it fell to the floor, then took his time working his way back up. Their limited time was probably a good thing. Her nipples were likely to pop off if they didn't get a reprieve, and while she didn't have a decent view of her clit, she had no doubt it was next in line. Every cell of her body was on edge around him. The good kind of edge. The kind that meant orgasm was about to happen.

He still watched her, and she realized two things. One that, he still wore pants. Two, that she'd never before undressed him. She did that now, easing her fingertips to touch his belly while he sucked in a quick breath. She took her time with the button, figuring he was past due for a little tortuous anticipation. When the zipper was down, she reached into his pants and wrapped her hands around him. Both hands. With room to spare. He hissed a breath, but when she looked up at him he managed to pry his eyes out of the back of his head and offer a grin.

She stroked him a couple of times, enjoying the stretch of silken flesh over steel. "Did I really do this to you?"

"Nonstop."

"What are you going to do tomorrow?" she teased. The words escaped before realized how much they didn't need to be said.

His eyes flashed dark, but just as quickly returned to what had become a molten shade of blue. "Tomorrow I'm going to have a hell of a kickstand problem. Tonight, I have the most beautiful, sexy woman ever to hit the Vegas strip."

She let his pants fall to the floor. "I highly doubt that."

He kicked the pants to the side. "Believe it. I do."

"I believe in you."

"Right now I'm hard to deny." He grabbed the sides of her head, holding her gently while he laid a fierce kiss on her. All the lazy *let's just stand here and be naked* had apparently come to an end. When he finally released her, her lips felt deliciously raw, and he was yanking sheets from the bed. The linens didn't stand a chance against that man's muscles, but they didn't go far. As soon as he'd cleared enough of the bedding for the two of them to fit on the exposed portion of the bottom sheet, he turned around and hoisted her to straddle his belly while he carried her to the mattress. He managed to lower her against the cool fabric with ease, and she didn't let him get away. He settled on top of her, his erection a prominent distraction pressed between them. "You feel that? *That's* real."

"I want you to look for what's real," she said. "When this is over, I mean. I want that for you."

"There's nothing else I want to find," he said. "Just be with me tonight."

"I thought that was my line."

He grinned and dipped his fingers between their bodies. "You're always so wet. I'm starting to think it's more of a medical condition than anything for which I should take credit."

"Trust me, it's all you. Now could you, I don't know, *use* it?"

He laughed and reached past her to snag a condom, then leaned to the side to roll it on. And on. And on. He was so huge, so thick, that she was practically panting by the time he'd sheathed himself. When he rolled back onto her, her legs were already apart.

He accepted the silent invitation without a word. Just sank into her.

She clutched his shoulders so tightly she left marks, and he started rocking against her, setting fire to her clit with every nudge forward. He muttered a string of profanity with which she fully agreed, then increased the depth of his strokes. Still so slow, so sensual. So deep. She felt the loss every time he left her and the unrelenting pleasure of his return. All while he kissed her neck, her breasts. Held her with strong arms. Watched her, blue eyes absolutely smoldering.

She threaded the fingers of one hand through his hair. With the other, she palmed his ass, urging the pace. He made a sound that sounded a little like *nuh uh* before shifting ever so slightly to the side, taking her with him. He snagged her higher leg behind the knee and almost decimated her with the new angle. He was so deep, pumping so much heat between her thighs that it was a miracle there weren't fire alarms going off throughout the building.

"Harder," she muttered. She hadn't any idea if he liked pillow talk, and at the moment didn't much care. The pressure of him filling her body was exquisite, and despite his relatively controlled pace, she was headed full steam for a meltdown.

"Harder?"

"Yes," she panted. "That headboard thing you were talking about?"

"Yeah." He managed to end up on his knees without missing a thrust.

"That thing where we wouldn't hear a knock on the door. Do that."

He shoved a pillow under her ass. "Do that?" he asked.
"Yes."

He withdrew slow, then slammed into her. "Like that?"
"Yes."

Rather than repeat, he just hung out. Ground against her clit. "You sure?"

"Yes. *Yes*."

He thrust hard again. Just once. "That angle okay for you?"

"For the love of all that is holy, *yes*."

Magic words. He finally listened. Finally wrecked her, hips pounding, the room echoing with the smack of bare skin. She was halfway gone when he lowered himself, changing the angle, adopting one that put *all* the pressure on her clit. She felt like she'd been shot out of a cannon when she came, delirious and dazed, her tightly wound body dissolving into bonelessness.

He kissed her neck, brushed her lips. Held her, still fully inside her. She might as well have been paper in the wind, for all the control she had left, but there was no mistaking his strength. His possession.

He released her leg, and she instinctively stretched, indulging for just a moment in the feel of the cool sheets against her hot skin. Then he tugged the blankets over his back and, like he had the night before, settled into her body. Into her soul. He kissed her. Made love to her. Took her for all she was worth, time and time again, like they had forever.

Like they didn't.

It wasn't until later, after he'd fallen asleep holding her tight in his arms, that her first tear fell.

And her heart ached, because she knew it wouldn't be the last.

Chapter Twelve

Jax woke before the sun, both arms wrapped solidly around Ellie. She slept with her head on his chest. Strands of her hair tickled his nose, and the way her fingertips curled over his lower belly made his chest ache. Her leg lay across his in quiet possession, her body laying claim to his. And his demanded to do the same.

Too much. It was too damn much. He needed to breathe. He needed air that didn't smell sweetly of her. He needed a space that wasn't hers and a time where he hadn't known her body. Hadn't known *her*. Because lying there next to her had him thinking all kinds of crazy things. Things that had no business in a two-day relationship. Scratch that…a two-day encounter. Because that's all this was. A couple of days of sex he'd regret for all the wrong reasons. Because in two days, she'd become close to him. As close as family. And when he realized that, he realized something else. The knot of pain he'd carried so long had eased. Seeing Ellie talk about her love for the mountains had changed something in him—made him see things Gracie's way. She and Ellie would have loved one another.

Would have. But they never got the chance.

It wasn't meant to be. Ellie would be gone soon. Too soon. And if there was one thing he'd learned from losing his sister, it was that he had no more capacity to mourn. He couldn't fit what Ellie meant to him into a box, but he knew however he defined this thing they had, it had to end. The idea that he couldn't protect her was more than a stupid supposition.

He'd proven it.

He'd failed to use protection. It didn't get more clear-cut than that.

From somewhere on the floor, his phone buzzed on vibrate. He was almost relieved. He made every attempt not to disturb Ellie as he eased from the bed. When he found the device, the display revealed it wasn't LVPD, as he thought, but Focker. Jax quickly stepped into the bathroom and pulled the door closed behind him before he answered. Focker wanted to see him as soon as was convenient. Leave it to Pretty Boy to think that was an appropriate reason to call at that hour. Jax dressed and paused long enough to write a note for Ellie, then he eased from the room.

And her life.

Closing the door didn't bring the relief he thought it should. The soft lighting in the hallway wasn't enough to ease the shadows from his mind. Or his heart. That she'd gotten in there to leave shadows to begin with tore him up all over again. He was nearly staggering by the time he hit the elevator. The hour, just past four in the morning, was about as close to quiet as Vegas ever got so he had the elevator to himself. He stood there, thinking about kissing her, until the doors slid open on his floor. He tapped out a quick text to Focker—*be there in fifteen*—and hit the shower. By the time he was dressed in his favored uniform of jeans and a tee, he felt almost human. But not right.

He'd eliminated her scent from his skin, but not her touch.

The urge to crawl back into her bed claimed him, but he kept walking toward Focker. Jax thought he'd break from the want of her, but that only fueled his fire. Whether or not she realized it, he'd let her down. He wasn't lost in the what-ifs. He had proof. Proof that, whatever she needed, he wasn't the man he should have been. Which meant that no matter how much he wanted to see where they could go, he wasn't the man for her.

He'd finally climbed out of that damned dark hole in which he'd lived for so long only to find himself staring at a sheer rock face, no way around. He'd found the sun, but he wasn't ready to move mountains. Not yet. And until he was, Ellie deserved more.

At Focker's door, he texted to let him know he was there before he knocked. The guy had been paranoid as hell from the threats alone. Now that he'd stared down the wrong end of a gun, getting through airport security with a stick of dynamite would prove less of a challenge than getting close to him. Jax didn't envy whoever worked his next gig.

Focker's manager opened the door and stuck his head in the hall, looking both ways before letting in Jax. He didn't greet him. Just waved him through.

Focker sat at a table in the suite, drinking a bottle of

mineral water or whatever it was he insisted kept his face youthful and complexion clear, but it didn't keep the worry away. He looked tired, and Jax wondered if he'd slept.

"Have a seat." Once Jax settled into the chair across from him, he continued. "I wanted to thank you for what you did out there."

"Just doing my job, but you're welcome."

"Not every man would consider that part of his job." He pushed an envelope across the table. "This is for you. The second half of your fee per our contract, plus a bonus."

"I appreciate it," Jax said. "But at four in the morning?"

"I'm prepared to offer you a job, Mathis. Full time. Look in the envelope."

Jax peeled back the flap until his eyes rested on the amount of the check. It was more than double what he was owed.

"The check is yours whether you take the job or not, but to be clear I'm offering that much a week, plus all expenses. It's around the clock while I'm traveling, but even then you're guaranteed ten hours a day of downtime. When I'm at home, you'll only have to accompany me to public events. The details will be in the contract, of course."

The number swam in front of Jax. He was stunned, and not just because Focker had managed to string together more than ten words in a sentence. A month, maybe two of the gig with Focker would pay Jax's expenses for a year. It was a hell of an opportunity, and he couldn't be in a better position to take it. He had nothing keeping him in Vegas, and moving out would be shutting the door on Ellie for good. He'd *have* to put her out of his mind then.

But he'd be running.

And he was done with that.

He might not be the man Ellie needed, but at least now he knew enough to try.

He stood, as did Pretty Boy. "Mr. Focker, I'm flattered by your offer, but I'm afraid I'll have to decline. I have a few things to work out here before I could commit to something of this magnitude."

Focker frowned, but reached to shake Jax's hand. "I understand. If you ever need a job, call me."

"I will. And next time you're in Vegas, feel free to look me up."

"I'll do it. Thank you."

Jax nodded to Focker's manager and left the room. Another door shut at his back. Another resounding click. Two doors closed in one predawn morning.

He stood in the hall for a long moment. Thinking about Ellie. Thinking about the note he'd left. Second thoughts burned like whiskey, but he held his ground. She deserved more.

And after the way he'd left her, he deserved whatever he got.

• • •

Something was off. Ellie knew it the moment she opened her eyes, before she officially realized she was alone in the bed. The warmth that had been there all night was gone. Telltale sounds from the bathroom were nil, the door open. By the time she rolled over to see Jax's clothes were no longer strewn on the floor, she had a knot in her chest as solid as the Rockies.

You. Did. Not.

If he were gone…well, then what? Nothing. She'd be back on the plane, just like she would have been anyway. Just as he'd so eloquently pointed out before he'd spent the night effectively ruining her for any other man.

And then he'd left.

She fell back against the pillows. Something ruffled on the table beside the bed, catching her eye. She reached over and snatched the paper, knowing before she even looked that he'd just *Dear Janed* her ass. She spent a long moment looking at his handwriting, learning this new piece of him, not reading what the words read. Not wanting to.

From the moment I laid eyes on you, I wanted you. Felt like I always had. And I tried, Colorado. I tried to be who you needed, but I can't protect you. Not even from myself. Especially not from myself.

She looked up. Blinked back more tears. She wasn't a crier, and damn him for making her one.

You deserve more than I have to offer, and God knows if you're pregnant, so does our child.

Shocked, she dropped the page. Her mind raced. *If you're pregnant.*

Shit. They hadn't used protection in the hallway, and she wasn't on birth control. How had she missed that? Frantic, she scrambled for her phone and pulled up the app that tracked her cycle. *Petals.* She was right in the middle of petals. What did that mean?

What the hell had been in that punch?

She hit a few wrong links before coming up with an explanation for the flower parts clogging up her cycle. *Fertility.*

Her hands fell to her stomach. *Holy. Shit.*

Stunned and shaken, she picked up Jax's note.

I hope you'll let me know. I hope you'll let me support you both in the only way I can.

Money? Was he really dismissing her with an offer to pay up? Did he really think they could create a *baby*, and he'd just walk away?

Did he really think she'd *let* him?

She picked up her phone. Pulled up his number and hovered over the delete button, but changed her mind. She switched to the picture they'd taken after she'd won the slots. Ignored the pain in her gut, because she was done. If the night before hadn't convinced him of anything, there was no point in trying.

She dropped the phone and picked up his note. She painstakingly folded it into a paper airplane, then threw it. It glided gracefully across the room, then hit the window and plummeted.

Her and Jax in a nutshell. Couldn't have summed it up any better than that.

She pushed her hair out of her face and climbed out of bed. Standing proved more difficult than she expected. She was sore. *Sore*, for heaven's sake. Moments from the night before flashed, rapid fire. The gunman. Jax diving for the guy like he had nothing to lose. Yelling at him in the hallway, then the most amazing wall sex ever had by anyone. Just the thought sent need ricocheting through her. Despite the unbelievable stupidity of not using a condom and the fact that the man in question was now on her shit list, the memory made her hot. All that anger and frustration had funneled into unbelievable passion — one she'd crave pretty much forever. And the continuation in her room had been incredible.

He was everything she could ever want in a lover, and now he was gone.

Gone.

And he hadn't even sent breakfast.

She glanced at the time. Her flight left in three hours. She wondered if he knew, then decided it didn't matter. It would take some getting used to. Even if she wasn't pregnant, he'd be with her for a very long time. She suddenly had a very unique, if shallow, understanding on why he kept Gracie so close. It was probably less of a fear of moving on than a fear of losing her. Already Ellie worried her memories of Jax would slip away, and knowing they'd never make another one only amplified that fear. Clinging to them wouldn't do anything but make her miserable. Miserable and needy.

God, how her body ached.

She thought of little else as she dragged herself to the shower and stood under a hot spray. The pounding water eased some of the soreness, but some of the pain went bone-deep. She lathered the soap and rubbed it against her skin, knowing his mouth had touched every inch. Knowing he'd possessed her like no man ever had. Knowing she'd cry for him like she had no one else.

And that was when the bottom fell out. Las Vegas was probably under some kind of water shortage—it usually was—but she let the water run until she was out of tears. Then she shut down the shower, wrapped herself in a towel, and applied cold washcloths to her face until she no longer looked like the spawn of the Michelin Man and the Pillsbury Doughboy, if such a thing could exist. By the time she was dressed and packed, she almost felt human. Emphasis on the *almost*.

She checked out of her room. She tried not to see the restaurant where they'd shared a table or the bar where he'd gotten all territorial over a Blue Hawaii. She astutely avoided the valet, because she knew where that had led. She averted her eyes from the reflecting pool, because it only reminded her of yet another time he'd been lodged between her thighs, that time on his shoulders so she could see the show. That the moment had been playful didn't help. Truth be told, *just sex* would have gone down a lot better.

She was stuck on the irony of that when, on the sidewalk near the carriage-spewing fountain, she saw him. Jeans and a T-shirt, tribal tattoo peeking from the sleeve. Sunglasses hid the direction of his ice-blue gaze, but she knew it was on her. Knew he watched her as she snagged a cab. She thought about waving like she was over him. Thought harder about sending him a *fuck you* text because she wasn't. But in the end, she just left.

And he let her go.

Long after her plane left the runway at McCarran and leveled off, en route for Denver, she finally faced the bitter truth.

What happened in Vegas didn't stay there.

Not by a long shot.

Chapter Thirteen

Taylor stirred her coffee and leveled her best schoolmarm look on Ellie. The youthful blonde didn't have a prayer of pulling off the grumpy elder persona, but Ellie appreciated the attempt. Sort of.

"Call him," Taylor said. "Text him. Do *something*."

She shook her head and gripped her cup with both hands. Three nights in the desert had made her soft. More than a month after leaving Vegas, she still couldn't shake the chill. Couldn't stop seeing fiery sunsets and pale blue eyes. Wanting warmth. "Nope. He made himself clear."

"Which is probably why he feels like too much of a jackass to call you," Taylor shot back. "So you call him."

"Because it's just that easy."

"Sarcasm doesn't suit you, El. And neither does this

funk you've been in for the past few weeks." Taylor softened her voice. "He has a right to know."

"I think he gave up his right to know anything when he ended things via a note on hotel stationary."

Taylor shrugged. "At least he didn't do it with a text message."

Ellie rolled her eyes. "At least. But I'd like to point out the fact that you just killed your whole *text him* argument. Some things just need to be said out loud."

Taylor's gaze narrowed. "Which kind of kills your argument to not say them."

Ellie shook her head and willed away the heat that threatened her eyes. She wasn't going to cry over him. Not anymore. "You don't understand. They were said. They were said and said and said. It was just a weekend thing. A crippling, mind blowing, orgasmic weekend thing, and it's over."

"Suit yourself," Taylor said, though she didn't sound the least bit convinced. "But two things. First, I'm going to stop listening to this. Like, yesterday."

"Kind of makes point number two moot, doesn't it?"

Taylor glared. "Nevertheless, point number two. If you don't talk to him soon, I'm going to fly to Las Vegas and kick his ass until he agrees to come back here to listen to what you have to say."

"How very ladylike of you," Ellie said dryly.

"Says the woman who got screwed upside down and sideways just a few feet from a crowded ballroom *and* half the Las Vegas PD."

Ellie's face heated. "*Half* might be an exaggeration."

"Whatever. Call him."

She didn't argue, mostly because there wasn't much

point. Unless Taylor had one. Maybe he was having second thoughts and hadn't said anything because of the way they'd left things. Because they'd both said all along it was just for the weekend. Or maybe he was just waiting for her.

"You can keep right on waiting," she muttered.

"Talking to yourself?" Taylor's voice sounded from across the coffee shop.

Ellie hadn't noticed her friend had left the table. Maybe it was the thin air. A lack of oxygen had to have an effect on a person, not that anyone else seemed all that affected. Sheesh. One weekend in Vegas and weeks later she still hadn't recovered.

Her gaze skated around the room. Midafternoon, the place was surprisingly empty. Although for February, the weather was pleasant. Below freezing, but not below zero. It was a great day for skiing, but Ellie was off that day, at least from the slopes. Instead of sitting at home in Minturn, she'd driven to Vail to meet Taylor on her break, and she'd brought along Murphy so he wouldn't destroy her house in her absence. She watched through the glass as he ran circles around one of the local kids, who laughed and tried to out-spin him. Considering the pace at which the leash wrapped around the kid, it looked like the dog had the win.

"I've got to get back to work," Taylor said. She, too, had turned her attention to the out-of-doors. "Nice day for the slopes. The ER is probably hopping."

"You're so morbid."

Taylor smiled sweetly. "I prefer practical. You coming with?"

"Just to the doors. I can't take Murphy inside the hospital."

The smile disappeared behind a mock scowl. "You need to take him to the loony bin. I swear I've never seen that mutt sit still."

"Speaking of which," Ellie said with a grin, "when is your date with the delivery guy?"

"Friday. Might be awkward, though, seeing as how he's already heard me passionately yelling over how a body like that had to be smokin' in bed."

Ellie burst out laughing. "You included that in your rant to a dog? One who was cowering?"

Taylor shrugged. "What can I say? It was an impassioned speech. Besides, it needed to be said."

As Taylor spoke, the kid in charge of the dog hit the sidewalk and Murphy pounced. The two rolled in the snow along the edge of the walkway, the kid laughing and the dog's tongue lolling. "Great," Ellie said of the kid. "He's going to be soaked when he gets home. His mom is going to kill me."

"No she won't. You're the only one crazy enough to babysit for them."

Ellie laughed. The family had eight kids, and Taylor had a point. Two for two, not that the one about Jax counted. Ellie sighed and pushed back from the table. She was glad her cup was still full. It wouldn't stay hot long outside, but it was better than nothing. Something had to keep her warm.

Outside, kid and beast were more tangled than she expected. She handed Taylor her drink and went to work, but the retractable leash had somehow ended up fully extended and was in knots. "What did you two do?" she asked as she tried to extract little Matthew from the tangled nylon strap.

The boy shrugged with all the innocence of childhood.

Made her ache inside, to think of Jax and his note.

"I'm not sure what happened," Matthew said.

Murphy barked. Whether in agreement or dissidence, Ellie wasn't sure.

"You can see the guilt all over his snout," Taylor said. "The dog, I mean. Not the kid."

Ellie blew a frustrated breath as Murphy ran yet another circle, further worsening the mess. The leash was wound so thoroughly around Matthew's arm that she'd never get it undone with Murphy bouncing around. "I'm going to have to unhook the leash. Murphy, sit."

The dog sat, but not convincingly.

"I mean it," Ellie warned.

Murphy yawned, and his tongue never made it back in his mouth. He sat there, tongue hanging out in the freezing air, like he hadn't a clue.

"Idiot," Ellie muttered. "Here goes nothing. Murphy, *stay*."

She unclipped the leash and started unwinding it from the kid, keeping one eye on the dog. He sat serenely…at least long enough for her to get almost as tangled in the leash as Matthew. Then his butt started to wriggle, and pretty soon he was on his feet.

"Murphy, *sit*."

He lunged like she'd ordered it, his unruly mixed-breed hide bounding joyfully through the snow.

Ellie's hands were all but tied. Literally.

Taylor dropped the coffee making a grab for him and missed. "Shit…er, crap."

"I've got him," Ellie said, disengaging as quickly as she could. "Help Matthew, would you?"

Taylor shook off the coffee that had splattered her and

went to work.

Ellie turned in time to see Murphy take off after a rabbit. *Great.* She responded with a shrill whistle. To her surprise, Murphy stopped, then turned and tore back across the snow toward her.

"Must have cold feet," Taylor said. "Either that or that dog has some sense after all."

Ellie barely heard her. The sound of an approaching car caught her attention, and with horror she realized it was moving fast. She tried jumping and waving, but the driver didn't appear to notice her. The dog didn't seem to notice the car. *Oh, God.*

Ellie darted across the road at the same time Murphy did.

No time.

It was her last thought before a bone-crushing impact brought her to her knees.

Chapter Fourteen

Jax had been playing quarter slots, two dollars at a time, for the better part of a month. It was ridiculous, really, but he found a semblance of peace there. Not much, but he'd take it. He didn't have much else to do. Focker was back to wherever cover models did their thing, and Jax had gotten some kind of citizen's accommodation for tackling the gunman. He'd barely looked at the paper before tossing it on a pile of junk mail keeping the dust off his end table, then proceeded to turn down every job offered him. He had money, didn't need it. What he needed was the drive to go out there. Risk everything.

What he needed was Colorado.

He needed a mountain to climb.

Her words haunted him. So did her touch. Her eyes. Her fucking uterus. He couldn't work—not like that. Not wondering if he might leave the world with his kid in it. He'd googled and now knew more about fertility than he ever cared to. Enough to know that Ellie should have known within two or three weeks of leaving if she was pregnant with his child.

And he'd counted five.

He'd dreamed of her every night. Sometimes of losing her, but mostly of holding her. Holding on. But he'd left her a note, and then he'd watched her go.

He'd fucking watched her go.

Every thought of that moment nearly killed him. At the time he thought he was being strong. Thinking of someone other than himself for once. Making a sacrifice. Maybe he was and maybe all that was true, but no amount of rationalization changed the fact that he'd let her go. Hadn't fought. Hadn't tried.

Just *watched*.

He'd given up bacon. Had a new favorite T-shirt, but he didn't wash it. Didn't wear it. Just kept it on his pillow, inhaling her scent. He hadn't been back to the park since the day the sunset had filled her eyes. He thought about going back, but knowing she wouldn't be there made it impossible to put one foot in front of the other. He was done with the desert.

The mountains called him. He thought about one in particular and wondered how he'd feel up there now that the view had changed. The ache in his heart demanded he find out. But he needed Ellie.

He stared at the machine in front of him. In all his years there, he'd never quite figured out which pictures constituted a jackpot and which a loss. The days of three pictures calling the shots were long gone. Now dozens of images crowded the screen, none of them meaning anything to him.

Nothing did.

His phone dinged. He almost didn't check.

But he did.

Colorado, the screen read. He clicked the notification and her message filled the screen.

At the emergency room. Bad news. Don't want to be alone. There are some things I should say. Can we talk?

He stared at the words, and in one brief second he translated them a thousand different ways. But only one thing mattered.

Ellie needed him.

He didn't stop to cash out his credits on the machine. Didn't go home to pack. Just ran out of the casino and grabbed the first cab he saw. On the way to the airport, he searched flights. The next one to Vail was six hours via fucking Dallas, but he could be in Denver in less than two. He booked it via his phone. If he didn't miss the flight, he'd be on the ground in two and a half hours. He'd rent a car and be…where? He couldn't remember where she lived—only that he'd never heard of the town—but he knew she worked in Vail. He'd start there. He'd have a two hour drive from Denver, but he'd need the time on the ground. That particular come to Jesus moment was long overdue.

Overdue, but it wouldn't be easy.

Curbside at McCarran, he paid and tipped the cabbie and hot footed it to check in. The line was blessedly nonexistent but the ticket agent was talkative. He bit his tongue. At some point she realized his plane was going to leave the gate at any minute and finally let him through.

He made it past security. Boarded the plane with nothing but his wallet and his cell phone. He must have looked crazy enough all strung out on coffee and memories that if anyone was supposed to sit next to him, they didn't. He wasn't even wearing a jacket. Not ideal for Denver in February—let alone a few thousand feet higher in Vail—but there was nothing that could happen when he got there that would leave him caring if his arms were cold. Either Ellie would want him or she wouldn't. Regardless, the weather would be the least of his worries.

Not until the plane ate up the tarmac and lifted off did the enormity of what he was doing hit him. Two months ago, he couldn't have imagined anything important enough to get him back to Colorado. Back then, stepping a toe across the state line would have brought him to his knees. Going to the mountains wouldn't have happened. Not for any reason.

Now he had one, and he just hoped it wasn't too late to tell her.

From the air, despite the miles between them, the desert morphed into the snow-covered Rockies far too quickly. He looked at the peaks without seeing them, wondering which one was Gracie's without really wanting to know. When he closed his eyes he saw that red hat disappearing under the churning snow and ice.

When he opened them, he saw Ellie.

The woman he loved.

He fucking loved Ellie.

And he'd lost her. He'd more than lost her…he'd pushed her. Watched her go, too afraid of what he felt for her to try to stop her from leaving.

And then what? The words had been his mantra, day in, day out. Everything he wanted to say, wanted to do, had always ended up in that same place. *Then what.* Because he couldn't change who he was. Couldn't change what he'd lost. The more he wanted her, the more he realized he didn't deserve her. But damned if anyone else did. No one could love her like he did. He made a mental note not to lead with that. It sounded stalkerish and a little creepy, especially if he hit his knees and started begging.

But first she had to be okay.

The plane touched down in more of a controlled wreck than an actual landing. The pilot, who had clearly missed his calling as a Las Vegas cab driver, joked over the intercom about the thin air in the Mile High City and made Jax exceptionally happy he hadn't booked a return trip. He didn't think his stomach could handle it. *Yeah, just stay here.* Where he'd lost Gracie.

Where he stood to lose Ellie. Maybe he already had.

After he cleared the jetway, he rented an SUV and pointed it west. He had one stop to make, and he made it count. Then he hit I-70, cursed the construction all the way to the city line, and then pushed the hell out of the speed limit. The road, four lanes winding at steep inclines through sheer rock faces and blankets of snow, should have been his worst nightmare, but it was the unknown at the other end of his journey that got to him. He wondered if she'd texted him again, but he didn't dare look. Not with his tires eating up the miles at breakneck speed.

By the time he found the exit for the hospital, his heart was in his throat. And he wasn't even sure it actually was the right exit for the right hospital…just that there was a chance.

He prayed Ellie was okay. Even if she hated him, he just wanted her to be okay.

He found a parking spot halfway occupied by plowed snow and parked there anyway. Exiting the SUV required equal parts skill and luck, but he managed not to break his neck on the way to the pavement, after which he sprinted to the building. He tore through the emergency room doors, nearly knocking an EMT off his feet. Over on a bank of waiting room chairs, a kid started crying. The god-awful smell of antiseptic and cleaning chemicals assaulted him. He barreled toward the admissions desk. "Ellie Montgomery. Where is she?"

The young blond woman at the admissions desk gave him one of those long, slow looks that belonged in chick flicks and romance novels, and most certainly not in emergency rooms. "Well, hot damn," she said after a moment. "You're Vegas."

More of an accusation than a statement. But clearly she knew about him, which might work in his favor. Or maybe not. The light bulb went off. "You're Taylor."

"Way to read my name tag, genius. Ellie's not here. Which kind of begs the question, why are you?"

"She told me she was in the emergency room," he said. "She works here, so I assumed she'd *be* here."

"She volunteers here," Taylor corrected with absolutely no angst in her voice. "She works on the mountain. And wrong emergency room."

He fought for patience. Ellie had to be okay, or her friend wouldn't be giving him hell. Unless Ellie wasn't okay...*especially* if she wasn't okay because of him. "How many can there be around here?"

She crossed her arms and hit him with a masterful glare. "At least one more."

"Which hospital?"

"Why should I tell you?"

"Because she sent me a goddamn text, that's why!" Several people turned to look. The kid had stopped crying to stare. The woman with him wore a death glare. Across from them, an old woman's brow disappeared into her blue hair. Jax bit his tongue. Lowering his voice a notch he said, "Look, I'm sorry. She sent me a text saying she didn't want to be alone. I'll show you if you want. Anything. Just please tell me where I can find her."

Taylor sighed. "I think this is the part where I threaten your balls if you hurt her, but I'm pretty sure the water under that particular bridge is mightier than the Colorado."

He stared evenly. "The Colorado River is a stream here—one you can cross on foot. What's your point?"

The woman tried to bury a smile and lost. "I almost like you, Vegas. But I'm serious. She's not in a good place right now, so if you barrel in there...wait. Why didn't she tell you where to go? Does she even know you're here?"

"No. And she's not going to if you don't tell me where to find her."

"She texted you and you didn't reply?"

"I came." The words clogged his throat. Questions followed. Was Ellie pregnant? Had she lost their baby? He wanted to ask, but he didn't want to violate her privacy. "I need to see her. Please."

The woman studied him for an endless minute, then sighed. "She's at this animal hospital. Head west." She scrawled a name on a pad of paper and tore off the sheet.

Reminded him of how he'd left Ellie.

Animal hospital. He blinked. "She's okay?"

"No, you asshole." Taylor glared, leaving no room to doubt what she thought of Jax. "She's absolutely *not* okay, but you'd know all about that, wouldn't you?"

Relief evaporated. "Thank you."

"Don't thank me. Just do right by her."

"That's the plan." He took the paper and took off running. After a harrowing climb back into the SUV, he searched the animal hospital and memorized the way to get there. Then he floored it...but only until he hit the legal speed limit. No point in wasting time on the side of the road in front of highway patrol.

He found the place within a few minutes. Managed a more conventional parking spot this time. And froze. This was it.

This was the rest of his life.

He snatched the keys out of the ignition, took a deep breath, and headed inside.

Chapter Fifteen

Ellie leaned back in the waiting room chair and tried to breathe. Murphy would be fine. A broken leg—certainly not a cause for relief, but it could have been worse. It had been a simple break, so if all went well and he halfway behaved while it healed, he'd get to keep his leg. He was out of surgery and doing fine, but she couldn't go home. There wasn't anything there for her except an empty house, devoid of everything but memories that didn't belong there. Murphy had at least provided a distraction. Without him careening around corners and tripping over his own legs, the silence would be agonizing.

The door chimed, followed by a rush of cold air. After sitting there for hours, she was well acquainted with what happened next. The dogs in the waiting area would start barking and anyone unfortunate enough to be holding a cat, sans the carrier, would get a lap full of claw marks. She didn't look up. Didn't need to see it again.

But something made her look anyway.

Right into the bluest eyes she'd ever seen.

"Oh, God. You're here." But even though she said the words, she couldn't believe them. She didn't move. Just saw herself running across the room into a mirage, because there was no way in hell Wolverine wanted anything to do with these mountains. Either she had the cruelest imagination ever, or...

"Colorado." Four syllables were all he said before he was in the seat beside her, his strong arms holding her like they never had before. Protectively, like he knew. Like he thought he could be that man he swore he couldn't. The emotional wall against which she'd leaned all day collapsed and the tears fell.

Sobs shook her, but still he held on. Not a word. Not a word needed. He just held her and let her cry. Finally she caught her breath. "You came?"

"Yes, baby. I came."

"You can't reply to a text?"

He laughed quietly and pulled back just enough to look her in the eyes. "Didn't seem like it would be enough. What happened?"

"My dog was hit by a car. He has a broken leg, but he'll be okay. I didn't mean for you...I didn't know you'd come. How did you find me?"

"I went to the ER, where apparently my reputation precedes me. I met Taylor, who quite clearly no longer thinks you're as lucky as she did that night at the hotel. Any chance you could call her off?"

She gave a watery laugh. "She doesn't listen any better than Murphy does, I'm afraid."

"Your dog."

"The one and only. Short for Murphy's Law, which pretty much sums him up. If something can go wrong, it will. I found him a couple of years ago with his tongue stuck to a light pole. Put up fliers and everything, but no one claimed him so I kept him."

"That actually happens?"

She nodded, still not quite believing Jax was there. "Yes. Every stupid thing that can happen has happened to that dog. As well as a few things that shouldn't."

"But he's okay?" Worry clouded his eyes.

"He will be."

Jax smiled, and while she believed it genuine, he seemed distracted. "Okay. Good. Can I get you some coffee or something?"

Oh, God. This was it. The part where he looked around, saw where he was, and was on the next flight out of there. It mattered that he'd come—it meant a lot—but soon he'd leave and she'd just have to get over him all over again. The realization hung heavily in the brittle air. "You did not come all the way here to get me coffee."

"No. I came to ask…" He looked around. Lowered his voice. "Are you…?"

She shook her head, her heart breaking. Was *that* was this was about? "No," she said. "I'm not."

"Good."

Her heart fell. Crumbled. A pregnancy wasn't ideal, but witnessing his relief firsthand tore what was left of her embattled heart. "You could have saved yourself a trip. I would have gladly told you that via text."

"No, that came out wrong. What I meant was good,

because I didn't want you to question my motivation for what I'm about to do." He looked toward the windows. Jagged peaks painted in late day sun made for a beautiful view for anyone else, but she couldn't image how much the view must hurt him.

And he'd come anyway.

"When I saw your text," he said, "I was terrified something had happened to you. That you were hurt. That you could have been...and lost it. And I just couldn't deny it anymore."

Her breath caught. "Deny what?"

His gaze cradled her. "I love you, baby. I know I don't deserve you, but I love you and all I want is the chance to show you that. Every day. You and your clumsy dog and your scary friend and even these goddamn mountains... whatever it takes, whatever I have to prove. I just want to be with you."

She smiled. Wary. Afraid to believe. "These mountains aren't going anywhere, you know."

"I know, and I get it. But I'm here. I'm here, and I'm not going anywhere either."

Ellie's throat clogged, and her heart soared, and still she was afraid to believe. "You don't have to do this."

He gave the slightest shake of his head and curled his fingers through hers. "If you think I was going to make it one more week without you, then I'm saying this all wrong. Because I can't. I don't want to."

Ellie wiped fresh tears from her eyes. "Taylor told me I should call you. That you had a right to know how I felt, but you watched me leave, and you didn't care. What I felt for you then didn't change anything. I didn't think it would now."

"Baby, I watched you go, and I died inside. I'm not me without you. Not anymore."

"Me too," she whispered. "And were an ass to leave me like you did. Hotel stationary has to be a new low."

He eased from the chair to the floor. "Understood, and in that respect I would like it noted I am on not one, but *two* knees."

"What are you doing?"

"Realizing how cold my hands are, for one. I can't feel my fingers."

"I know you're a tourist and all, but bringing a jacket to a ski resort in February is kind of a no brainer. Gloves are pretty much in the same category."

"Screw the jacket. I had places to go. Home wasn't one of them." He fished around in his pocket with his free hand and came up with a ring.

No box. Just a ring.

Ellie blinked.

"Jax…"

"Ellie Colorado Montgomery, winner of slots, eater of bacon, wearer of pancake syrup."

Despite the fact that she couldn't take her eyes off him, she couldn't help but notice a couple of heads swivel in their direction at that last part. "Easy now," she whispered through a fresh set of tears. "This is a small town."

"Not too small for pancakes, I hope. And breakfast in bed."

At this rate, there would be no controlling the water-works. "You do realize that no actual part of my name is Colorado?"

"Doesn't matter. What does Mathis do for you?"

Her heart settled in her throat. Did a few cartwheels. "Is that ring for me?"

He laughed. "God, I hope so. You saved me, Ellie. Somehow I don't think asking you to endure me for a lifetime is a fair trade, but I love you. I've spent the last five weeks counting the ways and the reasons. I love you, and I need you, and I just pray it's not too late. Will you marry me?"

Despite the obvious clue of the ring itself, she nearly fell from the hard plastic chair. "How could it possibly be too late? Of course I'll marry you."

"Really?"

"Really." She threw her arms around him, and he stood, lifting her. Spinning her around to the sound of applause. By the time he set her down, she was shaking. Dogs howled in the chaos. Somewhere in the room, at least one cat had to have drawn blood.

He slid the ring on her finger. "They didn't have one in the store that could outshine the sun," he said of the diamond, "but this one came close."

She held up her hand. A simple solitaire, if a rock the size of her knuckle could be considered simple. A band of gold that was a perfect fit. "Is this real?"

His face froze. "Of course it's real. The receipt is in the truck with the box. I just thought the box would be a little obvious in my pocket, but it's legit."

She laughed. "No, not that. You…here. Are you sure?"

Relief softened his features. "I'm sure. Never been more sure of anything. I love you."

She wiped away a fresh deluge of tears. The Colorado River had nothing on her. "I love you. I can't believe…I thought you said you couldn't come here."

"I'm here. I'm here until you kick me out." He leaned down and placed a whisper-soft kiss on her lips. "But if it's okay, there is one thing I need to do. There's a mountain not too far from here I'd like to visit. It's past time I climb it. Give myself a chance to see what's on the other side."

Ellie nodded, tears in her eyes. "I think Gracie would like that."

"Will you come with me?"

"Are you sure?"

"It's you and me, Colorado. Wouldn't have it any other way."

Hours later, when the morning sun broke over the eastern ridges, they stood together on the top of a mountain. Jax carried a red rose, Ellie a paper airplane.

And they threw them off the side of the mountain together.

Epilogue

Jax was nervous. Nervous wasn't a thing he did, but if the difficulty he was having with his cufflinks were any indication, he was in a world of trouble. "Are you sure you want to do this here?"

Ellie, some kind of ethereal sex goddess in a clingy white gown, stared at him in mock horror. At least he hoped it was a show, because he'd been on one of those *this is too good to be true* trips since they'd landed. "Are you kidding me? Where else?"

"Somewhere less *quickie*, perhaps?" He gave up on the cuff links and tossed them on the bed. He couldn't believe his life. Ellie had sold her former shrine to Focker in Minturn and they'd bought a place in Vail. She called it a chalet. He called it a pain in the ass to get up the mountain when the snow fell. But they both called it home, at least when they weren't in Vegas, and that was what mattered. Even the mutt liked it, but Murphy didn't have a grumpy bone in his body. If a dog could smile, the pooch never quit. Together, they were the closest thing he'd had to a family in a long time, but he hadn't stopped thinking of the baby they hadn't had. Especially after he'd called his mom. Sixteen years after she told him he was no longer her son, she cried when she heard his voice.

He had, too.

He'd also funneled his loss into something useful, teaching kids the finer points of pizza and French fries. The beginning ski positions took him back more than twenty years, when his kid sister had been so determined to out-ski him that she'd used her allowance to pay for extra lessons behind his back. For the first time since Gracie died, he welcomed the memories.

Thought of her and smiled.

You'd have loved Ellie, he told her. God knew he did.

"I happen to be quite fond of quickies," Ellie murmured, dragging him out of his thoughts and in for a kiss. "Especially with you."

He held out his hands and made a half-hearted attempt to back away from her. "I thought I wasn't supposed to wrinkle your dress."

"I thought you didn't care."

"I think that sounds like an invitation." He didn't wait for confirmation. Didn't give her a chance to argue. He lifted her to sit on the table, pushing the skirt of her dress out of the way until there was nothing between him and her spread legs but his zipper and a wet thong. He didn't know how anyone could wear one of those things, but he was glad she did.

"Consider it a demand." She went for his zipper. He went for his pocket. Ellie was allergic to something in birth control pills, so he'd been buying latex by the bucketful.

"Don't," she said.

"Don't what?"

"Don't use anything," she said a little shyly. "Unless you want to, I mean. But it's okay if you don't."

His heart soared. "Are you sure? You mean we could…?"

"Yes." No hesitance. Just his.

He stood there on weak knees while she took out his cock. Her hands on him were bliss. Cold, but so damn good. "We have fifteen minutes," she said.

"I'm going to need two. Maybe three." Hard as a rock, he pushed inside her, nothing between them but slick heat. *Fuck.* "Maybe one."

She fell back, landing on her elbows. Touched her own breasts. Moved her dress out of the way and tugged on her stiff nipples, just like he'd done a thousand times. Smiled sweetly.

Game on, sweetheart.

Seemed like they'd been there once before.

With a grunt, he dragged her toward him. Held her legs at just the right angle, and ground against her until all that tight, wet heat started to convulse around him. She abandoned her breasts to grasp uselessly at the polished wood tabletop. His balls sputtered protest, but he held out until some of her urgency settled into contentment, then he fucked her hard. Slammed into her until he thought the table would break. Had her calling his name all over again.

When he came, he thought he'd hit the floor, but there was no way he was missing the sensation of feeling her body surround his. He managed to pick her up and carry her to the bed before he collapsed, only to feel her mouth intimately on him.

"Quicker than a shower," she teased with a grin.

"In that case…" He flipped her over and returned the favor, lapping at her until he got so worked up he had to sink into her one last time.

One last time before they were married.

They were ten minutes late for their allotted fifteen-minute ceremony, but fortunately Elvis had yet to leave the building. They ran down the aisle, hand in hand. Jax's shirt wasn't buttoned all the way, and she was barefoot.

But she was still his fucking sun.

"Do you?" a scowling Elvis asked. Apparently *No Shoes, No Shirt, Bad Service* was a thing there.

"I do," she said.

Elvis turned to Jax. "Do you?"

"I do."

They traded rings to the music of an off key rendition of *Blue Hawaii* while being showered in fake casino chips.

And in every way that mattered, life began again.

Acknowledgments

Readers, YOU GUYS, you make it happen. Especially those of you reading all the way back here. And my street team. Seriously, people, I could not be more honored.

I also absolutely have to thank my former-but-not-old editor Kerri-Leigh Grady, who told me about the Vegas series. And then my most-of-the-time editor, Tracy Montoya, for saying yes, I should definitely do The Vegas. And props to I-can't-believe-she-hasn't-blocked-my-email-address Vegas right hand Robin Haseltine, who had the patience of a saint while I harassed her incessantly over all the Vegas series things. And of course to Liz, who helped me plot and bring this story to life.

AND THEN THERE WAS LISA. My awesome this-is-Vegas editor somehow got stuck with me for this book and has YET to stab me with a sharp object. (Or a dull one.) She's been a rock star, and I'm forever grateful for her attention to this manuscript.

I also have to credit my super cool parents who took me to Las Vegas when I was a teenager, which made me want to drag my city-hating husband there twenty years later. And he freaking loved it. So now we have a place, and how could I *not* write a book about our place?

And on that note, Michelle, you rock so hard. Thank you for being there for every word. You complete me. (I think you're the crazy half, but we'll keep that between us.)

And finally, to my future in-law (because our five-year-olds claim they are engaged and want twenty kids) and forever bestie, Melissa, who is probably so sick of hearing me talk about Vegas that she's likely in the fetal position right now as she reads this. One day, my friend, I'll have you out there on the Vegas Strip, even if I have to cram you into my luggage to make it happen. (Wait, is that weird? That wasn't supposed to be weird. Ah, well. You know what they say about Vegas…)

About the Author

Sarah and her husband of what he calls "many long, long years" live on the Mid-Atlantic coast with their six young children, all of whom are perfectly adorable when they're asleep. She never dreamed of becoming an author, but as a homeschooling mom, she often jokes she writes fiction because if she wants anyone to listen to her, she has to make them up. (As it turns out, her characters aren't much better than the kids). When not buried under piles of laundry, she may be found adrift in the Atlantic (preferably on a boat) or seeking that ever-elusive perfect writing spot where not even the kids can find her. Though she adores nail-biting mystery and edge-of-your-seat thrillers, Sarah writes in many genres including historical, contemporary, and supernatural romance and romantic suspense.

Find her @ www.sarahballance.com | http://sarahballance. wordpress.com | www.facebook.com/sarah.ballance.author. news | www.twitter.com/sarahballance | www.pinterest.com/ sarahballance34 | www.goodreads.com/author/show/4103362. sarah_ballance